Linda Berry started writing during the winter evenings of 2010 after hearing her partner's life stories for the one hundredth time and created her first book, *Nobody Said It Would Be Easy*.

Linda Berry wrote her second book, *17th Century Man* in 2011, and she only intended them for private use among her family and friends.

I would like to dedicate my book to my Gran. After all, she bought me my first notebook and pencil as a child. When I asked the question, "What do I write?" she told me to write down everything that I see and hear. "One day when you get old like me you can read what you've written and you will remember me and this moment. You should treasure this notebook and keep it safe because this moment will soon become a memory and you can keep it forever."

Linda Berry

17TH CENTURY MAN

AUSTIN MACAULEY PUBLISHERS™

LONDON • CAMBRIDGE • NEW YORK • SHARJAH

A CIP catalogue record for this title is available from the British Library.

ISBN 9781786290625 (Paperback)
ISBN 9781786290632 (Hardback)
ISBN 9781786290649 (E-Book)
www.austinmacauley.com

First Published (2017)
Austin Macauley Publishers Ltd.™
25 Canada Square
Canary Wharf
London
E14 5LQ

To my partner, Bryan J Royce for encouraging and
supporting me throughout the writing of this book,
for which I am truly grateful.

CHAPTER I

My name is Melissa Johns and my story starts when I move to a village called Peaty Hallow.

I am employed as a Maths and Music teacher at the Peaty Hallow primary school and was travelling each day by bus from a town called Speckleton for three years before I actually moved here. There is also a train service but travelling by bus is cheaper. Unfortunately the buses only run Monday to Friday.

Speckleton, my home town, is a small market town and up to about two years ago that's where I lived with my mother and daughter Evie. I started calling my mum Mother, because Evie was already calling me Mum so in order to avoid our little girl becoming confused we both agreed to do this.

I love my job and I get on extremely well with Janice the headmistress, and the other teachers Bernie and Phoebe. There are two other teachers who visit once a week. Joe teaches Art, and Ryan teaches Drama. The children here seem to be motivated and on the whole are quite well behaved. I've met most of the villagers who I know through the children who attend school.

During the week we run several short classes after school for children who feel they need extra tuition in Mathematics and English. One of the children attending my maths class is Thomas. who is one of Henry Walter's grandchildren. Usually he is quite attentive and bright, but over the past two months he seems to be somewhat distracted. I have often noticed him looking out of the window watching people go by.

Henry Walter owns The Lodge at the top of the village. The Lodge itself is magnificent and the Walter family have been residing there for years.

I went over to Thomas and asked if he was alright. He just shook his head and said, "I don't like living at Grandpa's. The Lodge is too big. It's scary. There are too many people living there and I miss my Mummy." Tears were pouring down his face and mucus from his nose. He didn't seem to have a hanky so I offered him mine.

Fiona, his nanny, came into the room and said, "Now young man, what's the matter? Why are you crying?"

"I want my Mummy. I want my Mummy."

"I've told you before, Thomas, Mummy has gone away for a while. So you must stay with your Grandpa. Now if you are ready," she put her hand out and Thomas took hold of it. Thomas left my handkerchief on the desk and was led out of school.

I remember three years ago when Ian and Thomas, identical twins, first started school. I was told that they had come to live with their Grandpa after Jeffrey's wife had gone away with Mrs Walter. Jeffrey wasn't able to care for his children because of work commitments. He runs his own construction company and travels around the country. He was forced to sell their home after a messy divorce and settlement. Jeffrey eventually moved back to The Lodge to be with his boys.

I did hear on the village grapevine that Mrs Walter had tired of her husband's philandering and had heard a rumour from some time ago, which was circulating around the village yet again, that Kim's son might belong to her husband. Apparently when she confronted Henry with what she'd heard, he totally denied ever having an affair with Kim. He doesn't understand why she's making so much fuss and why she's being so unreasonable. So one day, without any notice, she clears out their bank accounts and took some of the family's silver. She and her daughter-in-law are thought to be travelling around Europe on the proceeds. Kim is now the landlady of The Kissing Gate.

I do take Ian, for maths, but in a different class, and he doesn't seem to be having any problems. The boys would have been seven years old when they were moved to The Lodge.

Peaty Hallow is quite a large village, there are a lot of small businesses here and we also have a bank. There are two public houses, The Crooked Tree and The Kissing Gate, which I believe is named after the kissing gate at the front of the Community Centre. At the back of the centre there is a playing field and through the seasons some of the villagers play football, cricket and hockey. Some of the village events are held there, such as the village gala day and our school's sports day. The hall can be hired for celebrations and throughout the year there is an excellent choice of exercise and relaxation classes.

Janice, Frances, Trisha, Poppy and I usually attend an exercise class during winter when walking and other outdoor activities are hampered by the inclement weather.

On Thursday morning there is a small market held on the village green. Villagers don't have to rely too heavily on shopping at Speckleton because most items can be bought within Peaty Hallow.

I never intended to live here, it just seemed to happen.

One day Janice wanted to get some provisions from the local farm shop and she asked me if I would like to go with her. I wasn't doing anything in particular so we went in her car during our lunch break. The farm shop is quite large and it is part of a very large estate which is owned by Nigel and Linda Jack. The village post office is also located within the farm shop along with a bakery and a butcher. While Janice was doing her shopping I wandered around looking at some of the items on sale.

When Janice had completed her shopping I went over to help her with packing the bags. Frances was chatting to us as she operated the checkout.

"Mr Jack was telling me this morning that he's been advised by the estate agent to reduce the price of his cottage. It's been on the market for quite some time now."

"Yes it's a shame, because it's quite a nice cottage."

"While the cottage has been up for sale Mr Jack has tried on several occasions to let it, but it's unfortunate that no one wanted to stay. Lionel and Poppy are looking after the cottage and garden."

On the way back Janice pointed out the cottage. It was rather small but quaint and stood in its own grounds. I noticed the long front garden sweeping along a narrow driveway which leads up to the lane where we were. The first thought that passed through my head was that it would be well out of my price range. Janice pointed to the cottage next door and said, "That's where Frances and her husband, Brendan, and two children, Katie and Justin, live."

I made a note of the agent's telephone number and rang them after school. To my amazement it was well below the current market value but within my budget. I booked an appointment to view the cottage. Apart from having a reasonable sized kitchen, bathroom, sitting room and a small dining room, there were two reasonable sized bedrooms and a conservatory which was accessible through the kitchen. On the outside I found that there was a good sized vegetable garden and orchard at the back. Apart from the allotments which run alongside the driveway at the front the rest of the garden is completely private. After some negotiation and once all the necessary formalities were completed the cottage was mine.

When I asked my mother if she would like to move with me to Peaty Hallow she said she didn't want to move away from Speckleton. She and my father had always lived there. First and foremost she didn't want to move away from her circle of friends and activities. She has many happy memories attached to our family home. She reminded me that I was born and grew up there. She had nursed my father until he died there and latterly this was where my daughter and I lived when my partner, Neville, didn't want us anymore. She also told me she felt too old to move.

I asked Evie if she would like to move with me and she said that she was settled staying with her Nan and didn't want to move until she had completed studying pharmacy at Tinville University. At this moment in time she didn't want any disruption.

When I eventually moved into my cottage it felt so strange yet very exciting both at the same time. It felt so good to be independent and to have control over my own space. I had a freedom which I've never experienced before.

It has taken a long time for me to get used to being on my own and adjust to the sounds of the countryside. When I first moved here I was constantly being woken up at four o'clock in the morning by the dawn chorus, but in particular by a blackbird perched in one of my trees singing to his heart's content. Although I do like to hear the birds singing I didn't appreciate being woken up quite that early.

Also from time to time, I can hear cows bellowing after their newly-born calves for a few weeks on end. That's such a heart-felt noise because they know that they have given birth but they don't have calves. I did find out that the calves are taken from their mothers and hand-reared for veal. I find it very upsetting and find it much harder to get back to sleep once I've been disturbed.

I wasn't alone for long. I noticed a cat mooching around the garden. I tried several times to make friends with her but she would run off or climb one of the trees to get out of my way. I used to leave out my leftover meals and a bowl of water, just in case she had been abandoned in the lane.

One day I must have left the kitchen door open because I found her fast asleep on one of the chairs in the conservatory. At first she did not appreciate a lot of fuss.

She would glare at me as if to say what do you think you're doing? I did take her photograph and made a poster which I placed on the notice board in the farm shop, just in case she belonged to someone in the village, but no one came to claim her.

Now she's a different cat and when I'm relaxing in the sitting room or conservatory she'll sometimes jump on my lap, settle down and fall asleep. When she's like this we are friends and she is a lovely cat, but the other day she did annoy me big time. She brought home a trophy, a baby rabbit. She was so proud of her achievement when she dropped it on the kitchen floor. I thought it was dead.

Luckily she was thirsty so while she was having a drink, I very quickly scooped it up and ran up my driveway. Meanwhile the rabbit, realising that it had been saved, was trying to free itself. I leaned over the small stone wall into the allotments and released it. Within a few moments the rabbit was making its way towards the field adjoining the allotments.

Occasionally, when I'm out in my front garden weeding in the evening, I do see a few of the people working in their allotments. I know some of them by sight but not by their name.

I must confess that I do get help with the garden. There's far too much for me to manage by myself. I do love having a garden but my knowledge and skills are still very poor. Lionel, who also works for Henry Walter and Nigel Jack, comes once a week to manage the vegetable garden and the orchard.

The front garden is looking very pretty and the vegetable garden is well stocked. In the orchard there is a good variety of fruit trees and all are bearing fruit. There is another tree growing in the orchard. It's not like the other trees, it is unusual yet hideous. The trunk is crooked and its branches are twisted, bent and winding. Just a few months ago the tree came into flower which was very impressive to say the least. The fragrance was overwhelmingly pleasant and it was a mass with honey bees. The tree literally hummed. I don't know its name nor its origin but I find it fascinating.

The previous owner of the cottage, Nigel Jack, told me that he believed that the cottage was cursed. He had previously offered the cottage to let and a couple of tenants claimed they saw something come out from the shadow in a corner of the sitting room. Maybe it was haunted, I found myself thinking.

No! I don't believe in ghosts and there is usually a perfectly good explanation for most things that go bump in the night, but some of these sightings had been claimed to be happening during the day. So I am a tad sceptical. Up to now I have nothing to report but am keeping an open mind.

When the fruit and vegetables are ready Lionel harvests them and stores everything in trays which he stacks in one of the outbuildings. It's nice and cool in there so it's an ideal store.

"Why don't you have a go at making some jam or chutney, Melissa?" asked Lionel.

"Do you know I've never made any preserves before. Frances is trying to encourage me to make some jam. In fact she's left me copies of some of her jam, chutney and jelly recipes."

"It's not that difficult to do because me and Poppy have always made our own preserves. We've been doing it for years."

So one evening after tea I have a go at making some jam and chutney.

The next evening when in the orchard the twisted tree has what appears to be fruit hanging from its branches. On the ground there are some windfalls. I pick one up and on closer inspection the skin is brown, hard to the touch and wrinkled, as a fruit it doesn't look very appetizing. I'm curious to know what it tastes like so I take a batch back to the kitchen. I wash the fruit under the cold water tap I then puncture the skin with my teeth and some juice comes into contact with my tongue. The taste is extremely bitter and it instantly dries my tongue and mouth.

Beyond the hard exterior the texture of the fruit is soft, fluffy and clear and I wondered if it would make a good jelly. So I made a small amount of jelly which turned cloudy and didn't completely set. I taste a little on a spoon and there is a distinctive flavour which I find pleasant. It's not too sweet nor too sour. I don't know why but I add this so-called jelly to jam already made which was set aside to cool slightly before transferring into jars. I decide to name this jam Melissa's Special Jam.

There was a little left in the bottom of the pan so I scraped it out and spread it onto a piece of toast, it's delicious. This is the best part of making preserves. The special fruit seemed to enhance the flavour of the other fruit that it's mixed with. So the following evening I collected more of the special fruit and repeated the process. When I look at all the jars on the shelf in my pantry I feel so proud of what I have achieved.

On the spur of the moment I took a jar of my special jam around to Frances. She was surprised because even though she had been trying to encourage me to make jam she didn't think I would.

Next day at school I gave a jar of my special jam to Janice. Apparently her mother makes jam and I was interested to know what they thought of it.

CHAPTER II

Today is the village's Gala Day.

The weather is being kind and is looking good. The sky is blue and the sun is shining and I feel great.

Mother and Evie are coming today by train, and they're staying for the weekend. The pair of them should arrive at the station at about twelve noon and they will be getting a taxi to my cottage.

Yesterday, Poppy came to help me clean the cottage. Life's been a bit hectic lately and I haven't had time to be thorough around my home. Mother is bound to find something that's been missed. Honestly, Evie is just as bad, she winds us both up when she feels like it. I'm not completely sure about my mother either. For all I know she too could be winding me up. So I'm not taking any chances, anything for a quiet life, that's me.

Ben, one of Nigel Jack's sons, very kindly brought a parcel of mine from the Post Office yesterday afternoon on his way to the doctor's surgery. The surgery is nearly opposite my cottage and he was taking his wife, Iris, for a routine check up. She's expecting their first child later on this year.

Gala day is organised by the Community Centre committee and both Henry Walter and Nigel Jack are on the committee.

The Gala day parade starts from The Lodge travelling along a designated route and finishes on the field at the back of the Community Centre. Everyone taking part will meet at The Lodge. Henry Walter leads the procession driving his vintage car, accompanied by his son, George, and two grandchildren, Ian and Thomas, followed by the Peaty Hallow marching brass band. This year there are ten floats being entered and they form a line behind the band.

This year's theme is Months of the Year. Our school's float entry is July, Down on the Beach. Bernie, Janice, Joe, and Ryan have been very busy coaching the children taking part. All the children in the entire school have been working for weeks in their art classes on the scenery boards for the float today. There were too many volunteers this year so all the names were placed into two boxes and I was asked to pick out seven names from each box. Only ten children will be going on the float with four children in reserve just in case some change their mind or are ill at the last minute. Joe and Ryan will be a part of the scene and will travel with the children to ensure everyone stays safe.

Flight Lieutenant Steel, a close friend of Henry Walter, will be flying over The Lodge in his Mustang to officially open Gala day. My cottage is along his flight path so I should hear and perhaps might see the plane, that's if I'm in the garden when he flies past.

Mother and Evie have arrived. My driveway is too narrow for the taxi to come down as there isn't enough room for it to turn around. As I'm making my way up to the top of my driveway to greet them, I find Mother paying the driver and Evie is taking their cases out of the boot.

"Hello, you two. How lovely to see you. Come here," and we all have a family hug.

"Hi, Mum."

"Hello, dear."

"Let me take your case, Mother," I offered.

"No I can manage, dear."

"Did you both have a good journey? You seem to be on time."

"Yes, it made a change for me to come on the train. We didn't have to negotiate any steps nor any inconvenience caused by traffic."

As we were walking down the driveway we could hear a cockerel crowing continuously but it doesn't sound like he's saying cock-a-doodle-do. He's screeching very loudly and now it sounds as though he's got a sore throat and he's struggling to reach the required note.

Evie says, "It's the wrong time of day for that. Isn't it? He should be crowing early morning, not at lunch time. There must be something wrong with his body clock. Mustn't there?"

"You're in the country now where things don't always go according to plan," I reply.

Just then Mr Ellis' racing pigeons fly above our heads. I just mention to Mother and Evie that Mr Ellis has just let them out for a bit of exercise.

Just as we're going into the cottage Flight Lieutenant Steel flies over quite low. It's the first time Evie and Mother have seen his fly past. Last year they came on the bus, got held up in traffic, and missed it.

Once Mother and Evie have settled in we have a light lunch. I explain that there is a marquee set up in the Community Centre grounds and inside there is a dance floor and a seated area. A steel band is the first on the programme to play. The music will continue throughout the afternoon and into the evening with a variety of performances of groups and bands from all over the county. I also mention that I've entered two pots of my special jam in the WI newcomers' section just to get into the spirit of things.

After lunch, Mother, Evie and I walk down to the Community Centre. We can hear the steel band playing and Mother decides to go into the marquee to listen to the music. Evie and I went into the centre to have a good look around.

Inside the hall it's a hive of activity, including the usual guessing games like name of the doll, the weight of a cake, how many marbles are in the jar. Evie and I have an attempt at all of them.

Frances and a few other ladies from the village have set up in the kitchen and are providing hot and cold drinks and a variety of snacks. We give her a wave and smile as we walk by and she reciprocates.

One of the pubs from another village is providing a bar, I forget which one. There are tables and chairs set up inside and I spot Trisha and Harry. So we go over and have a quick word. They have one son called Danny who comes to the village school. They both work at Tinville University and they are both Evie's lecturers.

"Hello, how are you both?"

"Yes, we're fine thanks, Melissa. Hello Evie, how are you getting on with your dissertation?" asked Trisha.

"It's nearly complete, thank you. There are a few items I need to research but it's getting there."

"Good. I'll look forward to reading it next week."

"Where's Danny?" I asked.

"He's staying with his granny for the night. We'll be collecting him tomorrow," replied Harry.

"Yes, we've got the entire day to ourselves so we're making the most of it," added Trisha.

"Yes, that's right love, but later we're going to The Kissing Gate to take part in the Gala day quiz with Mr Walter."

"Anyway Evie, we'd better be getting back to your nan. She'll be wondering where we are."

"We'll perhaps see you later," Evie said.

On our way to the marquee I see children further up the field riding ponies and having a great time. They're probably from the riding stables at The Lodge.

Inside the marquee there is a real carnival atmosphere. The steel band is playing and there are a few people dancing. We find Mother sitting at a table and she's enjoying the music. She's really getting into the rhythm.

This afternoon, The Crooked Tree public house will be holding a darts tournament semi-final and final with its own darts team led by Mr Walter competing against The Kissing Gate team led by Mr Jack and two other public houses from two of the surrounding villages. Unfortunately I do not know which. Mother, Evie and I aren't really interested in watching the darts tournament.

The Kissing Gate public house, my local, is holding a Gala day quiz with its own team competing against The Crooked Tree and four other public houses from Ant on the Wolds, Beesford, Berryville and Furymarsh. All the team members are selected by their respective public house by a process of elimination; each time each player wins it is recorded. So the individuals that make up the teams here today are the strongest contestants of their pub. The people who represent The Kissing Gate are Bernie, Janice, Brendan, Lionel, Poppy and me.

It's time for me to leave so I say, "Cheerio for now, see you both later" and they both wish me luck.

As I expected The Kissing Gate is very crowded but I manage to manoeuvre my way over to Janice who has very kindly reserved our seats and table. Henry Walter and his team members, George, Trisha, Harry and two others are assembling adjacent to us. They all acknowledged me as I was sitting down. I respond with a smile and nod my head.

I ask Janice the names of the two I don't know and apparently they are Eamon and Lorna. Lorna's father is Flight Lieutenant Steel and that explains why I'd never seen them before.

"Where are the others, Janice?"

"They're all here, they've gone into the bar for a celebratory drink. Hey, our darts team won the tournament. Nigel Jack is over the moon, he just can't believe it. The Crooked Tree's team have never been defeated by The Kissing Gate. Oh Mum and I like your special jam by the way, not bad for a first attempt. Oh, you'd better have this."

To my surprise she presented me with a small certificate; my special jam came 3rd.

"What a lovely surprise, thanks. I'll go and congratulate our darts team later, providing I can get through to the bar."

The bell rings and everyone taking part settles down and the quiz begins. On the whole the questions don't seem to be that hard. At the end of the quiz all the answer sheets are collected and marked by Tracey, the official adjudicator elected by the Community Centre Committee. Within a few minutes the winning team is announced. Yippee! Our team has won. A few shout "fixed" and most of us have a laugh.

Kim is elated, this is the first time that The Kissing Gate has won a Gala quiz. She announces "Drinks all round" and everyone cheers. The two plaques will be engraved and hung behind the bar.

What a triumph.

I stayed with the other team members and joined the celebration of our victory. I did make attempts to go and congratulate our darts team but just wasn't able to negotiate my way through. The pub was full to overflowing and I needed to get some fresh air. I'm not usually claustrophobic but tonight I'm feeling a need for a wide open space. I only became aware of it while standing and inching my way through the crowd.

Once outside I take a few deep breaths of fresh air and I'm fine. It's still light and pleasant. I've arranged to meet Mother and Evie in the marquee.

Inside the marquee there's a local band playing and when I spot Mother she looks like she's had enough. She's beginning to look tired.

"Are you ready to go home, Mother?"

"Yes, let's go."

"Mother, where's Evie?"

"Oh a young man came over just a few minutes ago and asked if she'd like to dance. They're somewhere on the dance floor. I've lost sight of them."

"I wonder who that could be."

"I don't know, he didn't say. He looks a very nice young man. He's very well mannered. She'll be alright."

"Well, she's old enough to look after herself. Come on Mother, let's go."

I take hold of Mother's hand and we stroll arm in arm, chatting about this and that, up the main street and down the lane back to my cottage.

As we go by Frances' cottage her dog, Molly, runs up to the gate wagging her tail. We hear Brendan calling her as we go by.

We have our supper in the conservatory where it's nice and cool and listen to the blackbird singing in the orchard. There's another bird singing further up the lane but I'm not able to identify it. Mother says, "I think it's a nightingale."

I show my certificate to my mother but she isn't really that interested.

When we've finished our snack we admire the sunset and both agree that it's going to be another nice day tomorrow.

CHAPTER III

Mother and I have had a really interesting weekend. Mother spent most of Sunday pottering in the garden and finding faults with Lionel's method of gardening. We only saw Evie very briefly at breakfast before Charles, another of Nigel Jack's sons, came and took her out for the day. Mother tries some of my special jam and she takes a jar back with her. Evie returns about ten minutes before the taxi arrives. So she only has time to say that she has had a nice day on the estate with Charles and that they are going to keep in touch. Nowadays there's plenty of choice, but personally, I prefer talking to someone. She also mentions that he's an obstetrician and his work is linked with Brasham University.

It looks like it's going to be another nice day and I feel on top of the world. It's Wednesday and I'm going on the school trip today to a village called The Mound, which is approximately eighty miles away, and I've never been there before.

We always organise a trip for the children aged ten years old during their last term before they transfer to the Speckleton Grammar or High School in September.

There's a choice, a booked set lunch at The Hall or take your own picnic. I'm having a picnic down by the river, which looks quite near the centre of the village from the map which was supplied in the information pack, which Janice produced and sent to all the children's parents a few months ago. All the children going on the trip must be accompanied by a parent or guardian. Any children who are not able to go on the trip must attend school as usual. From the information supplied The Mound is a small but picturesque village unlike Peaty Hallow.

After lunch we will all meet in the village centre and wait for an escort to take us as a group to a working farm and museum. The children will be able to witness first-hand how a farm was run in bygone days. They will be able to interact with the staff, observe their costumes, see how they live and ask them questions. Janice thought this was an ideal situation for the children.

The coach will be picking us up by the village green at nine o'clock so I mustn't be late.

Janice did mention yesterday that Henry Walter and Flight Lieutenant Steel will be accompanying Ian and Thomas. They will also be responsible for Danny. His parents won't be able to go on the trip because they have to go to work. She also mentioned that Henry Walter and Flight Lieutenant Steel will be taking the boys to view the boarding school at The Mound as coincidentally it's their open day. Ian and Thomas will be educated at the boarding school following the family tradition. Henry Walter and Flight Lieutenant Steel met at this boarding school and have been buddies throughout their lives.

As I walk around the corner to join Main Street I see Harry with his three boys, Bradley, Dermot and Cameron, walking ahead of me. Bradley, Dermot and Cameron are triplets but they are not identical in looks.

Harry seems to be the leader and the boys are dawdling behind. He keeps stopping and very politely asks them to get a move on.

At the village green most of the children and their parents have already arrived. Whilst they are waiting for the coach Janice is checking to see who's missing. The coach arrives and everyone gets on board, except Janice and me. She just mentions that Brendan and Katie are missing to me and the driver. We agree to wait for at least another five to ten minutes. As Janice and I are boarding the coach Brendan and Katie are spotted coming towards the coach from the direction of the school.

Once Brendan and Katie are on board Brendan apologises and thanks everyone for waiting. He explains that Justin, his son, refused to go to school when his friends came to collect him. He wanted to go on the school trip so Brendan and Katie had to escort him to school to make sure he was going to stay.

I notice that Brendan went to join Harry on the back seat. It doesn't take very long for everyone to settle down for the journey. A few of the children get out of their seats, from time to time, to go and talk to their other friends. A few of them manage to swap seats for a while.

After two hours we see a village sign which says Welcome To The Mound. As we are approaching the village centre I notice a tree, which is identical to the one in my orchard, on the edge of the village and I take a note of the route.

When the coach draws to a halt the driver hands a microphone to Janice and she announces, "Right

32

everyone, can you just remain in your seat for a moment. Those of you going for a picnic please leave the coach first and remember that we will all be meeting here this afternoon at two o'clock. A guide will meet and escort us to the working farm and museum. The rest of you follow me in an orderly manner and we will go and have our lunch at The Hall. I also just want to say thank you to the driver for bringing us here today and we will all need to meet here again later at five o'clock. Thank you."

Janice returns the microphone to the driver and everyone going on a picnic starts to file off the coach. As I am getting off the coach I turn to Janice and said, "Cheerio Janice, have a nice lunch and I'll see you here at two o'clock."

By the time I get off the coach I notice Henry Walter and Flight Lieutenant Steel marching the boys up the hill.

I just follow the children and parents to the river and picnic area. I find a quiet place away from the others in the party. I just want to be by myself and sit on a bench under the shade of a weeping willow tree by the river's edge. While I have my map handy I just want to check the route back to the tree. I mark the route with my pen on the map so I won't forget or get lost. I check my watch and there isn't time to go exploring now but after the visit to the working farm and museum will be an ideal opportunity for me to go.

Our escort took us all around the farm and around a row of cottages. In the fields at the back we saw several people working using many different hand tools and some were hay making. In an adjoining field there are some working shire horses pulling machinery which is cutting the long grass and other shire horses were pulling machines baling it. I'd never witnessed a scene like this before, only from photographs which I'd seen as a child.

When we arrive at the museum there were several exhibition buildings, one of them was full of farming machinery from horse drawn to steam. There were a great variety of hand tools displayed on hooks along the walls. There were plaques mounted by each one with a detailed description of its use. They were displayed in date order. There were some framed black and white photographs of workers in the fields using the tools.

In another building there were two blacksmiths running demonstrations. One was putting a new shoe on a shire horse, the other was making knick-knacks. I found the gift shop and had a good look around. I bought some postcards, which were the copies of the black and white photographs I had viewed on the wall in the exhibition hall, as a souvenir of my visit.

I find my map and go in search of the tree. Eventually I find the tree in a garden of a guest house. I notice a sign which says:

Welcome to The Mound Guest House.
Also open to non-residents.

So I go through the gate and look at the tree. I notice a gentleman coming into the garden and he meanders over to the tree. He is short in stature and is very smartly dressed. He is wearing a straw hat and is carrying a black cane.

"I've got a tree just like this one at home. Do you know what it's called?" I asked.

"Yes, we call it a Tinsel tree," he replies, as he looks into my eyes. His eyes are icy blue which send shivers up and down my spine. It has been a long time since a man has looked at me like he did.

"Oh, at last I have a name, but it doesn't look anything like a Tinsel tree, it's not very pretty," I replied.

"No, but don't you find it fascinating?"

"Yes I do. In fact I made some jelly from some of the Tinsel tree fruit and added it to some jam which I'd made. It makes the jam taste so much better somehow."

"Does it indeed?"

"Yes it does, and I've even named it Melissa's special jam."

"I'm surprised you even attempted to make a jelly because the fruit of this tree doesn't look very appetizing and it's very bitter in taste. Do you live locally, dear?"

"I live in a village called Peaty Hallow."

"I know Peaty Hallow, we used to live there, but it seems such a long time ago. In fact, I know your tree, because it used to be ours."

"Oh, what a coincidence."

"Yes it is. What brings you to The Mound, dear lady?"

"I'm here on our school's day trip."

"What did you say your name was?"

"Melissa, and what do I call you?"

"Call me Frederick."

Frederick is quite a gentleman, he took hold of my hand and escorted me to a garden table, pulling out a chair for me to sit on.

"Thank you. You're a real gentleman."

"We treat our guests to Tinsel tree jam."

"Your guests! Is this your guest house?"

"No, my father and mother own it. They've been here for years."

He gave me a look. I can't find the words to describe it but it makes me blush.

"Tell me, Melissa, have you been through the kissing gate at Peaty Hallow?"

"Yes, I pass through it when going to the community centre."

"Community centre, that certainly wasn't there when we lived in Peaty Hallow, there was just a field where I used to play. I've kissed a few girls there."

"Oh, I've never been kissed there."

"Before you go I must give you a jar of our Tinsel tree jam for you to try. You may find the taste more intense than yours but I hope you will enjoy it."

"That will be nice, thank you."

Frederick was so charming, considerate and polite. I feel so comfortable in his company. I feel that I have known him for a long time. I can honestly say that I haven't met anyone quite like him.

Frederick led the way inside the guest house. It seems a little dark at first but when my eyes have adjusted, wow! I wouldn't be able to afford to take a break here, was the thought running through my head. I could hear someone playing a harpsichord. How delightful.

"I won't be long, Melissa, please feel free to wander around."

I am just inside the reception area which opens out into a lounge. There were some guests sitting having polite conversation. It is like stepping back in time. What a novelty.

I follow my ears in pursuit of the harpsichord music. I go down a long straight corridor and into a room. Oh, this must be the library, but I could still hear the music. It must be further down the corridor.

I can hear footsteps coming down the corridor and into the room. It is Frederick.

He gives me a jar of jam as promised.

"Thank you, Frederick. That looks good."

"Can we go outside?" he whispers.

I nod and we return to the garden.

"Enjoy your jam but spread it liberally. In a few weeks or so you should start to feel the benefit of eating it. The jam tends to affect people in different ways but you should start to feel stronger and have more energy. You can keep it for yourself or share it with others if you wish. One jar isn't going to affect you very much. As I mentioned to you before, we allow our guests to consume the jam while they are staying with us.

Guests don't usually stay here for more than two weeks at any one time. It tends to heighten that feel good factor that you get when on holiday. Once they return home the effects wear off. Our guests are not aware of the benefits of the jam, we tend to keep that a secret. I would like you to do the same. Do not use the jam generously because it will cause severe side effects like hallucinations, stomach cramps and severe vomiting. If you do like the jam just let me know, here's a card with my contact details."

"Thank you, Frederick." I take hold of his hand, look into his eyes and say, "I promise not to tell anyone and can reassure you, Frederick, that you can trust me." I put my little finger around his and whisper "promise."

He responds by taking my hand and caressing it softly with a kiss.

"Bye, Frederick, I've really enjoyed your company. I must go."

"Cheerio, Melissa. Have a safe journey home. Please let me know if you like our jam or not."

"I will. Bye."

I manage to find my way back to the pickup point and it looks like most of the children and their parents are already on the coach. I did begin to think that I was late but when getting on the coach found that Janice and a few others weren't on board.

After about ten minutes Janice, Henry Walter, Flight Lieutenant Steel, Brendan, Harry and their respective seven children boarded the coach. Everyone cheers as they get on the coach. They'd all been on the river trip and all thanked the driver for waiting as they filed by.

After Janice has settled herself down I turned to her and said, "Have you enjoyed your day?" and she replied, "Yes it's been an interesting one. This is a first for me.

I've never been late for anything in my life."

"What about you? Have you had a good day?"

"Yes, I have. It's been very interesting."

"Good, I'm pleased."

CHAPTER IV

I've already decided to keep Frederick's Tinsel tree jam
for myself, but I am continuing to give my special jam to
my mother and colleagues at work. After I've consumed
some of Frederick's jam I feel so energised. I feel great.

I've phoned Frederick several times and now he's
invited me over to The Mound to stay at The Guest
House for the weekend. I've already bought my train
ticket and I'm so looking forward to seeing Frederick
again. It's been a long time since I've spent the weekend
with anyone other than Mother and Evie, it'll make a
complete break for me. I feel like I'm going on holiday.
Nice. I've already packed my smaller wheelie suitcase
and I'm intending to walk down to the station providing
the weather stays fine. I've never been on the train to
The Mound. I've always travelled in the opposite
direction to Mother's. I will have to get someone to
prompt me when I reach my destination. I would hate to
miss my stop. I will also leave enough food and water
out for Moggie. I've already had a word with Frances
just to keep an eye on her, her food and water and my
cottage.

There have been several reports of attempted break-
ins just lately and two actual burglaries. There was an

40

article in last month's local parish magazine reporting about an unfortunate Mrs Brown who was woken up only to find a burglar standing right over her. She was terrified, so much so that she had a stroke during the early hours. She was found the next day by her carer who found her unconscious lying in the hallway. Fortunately she wasn't physically hurt by the intruder but lost several items of jewellery of significant and sentimental value. She's now thankfully recovering in hospital but unfortunately she wasn't able to give a description of the burglar. Another gentleman in the village, Mr Upton, who went out for the day with his family came home only to find that his home had been ransacked. He found his hamster, Joey, pinned to the kitchen wall. Its blood had trickled down and dried on the wall. He's having to stay with his son because he went into some kind of shock. His daughter is endeavouring to sort things out on behalf of her father. He's lost his confidence and is at the moment too scared to return home.

Once I am out of the station I notice a horse-drawn carriage and horse-drawn cart and on the sides of both is inscribed 'courtesy of The Guest House.' Lovely. I hand my wheelie to the chap that seems to be in charge of the horse and cart. I then make my way over to the carriage; because it is such a nice day the canopy on the carriage is folded down on one side. I sit down, which to my surprise, is extremely comfortable. This is the life.

"Excuse me, Madam, just letting you know that we're waiting for four others. I'm hoping they won't be too long."

"That's fine. I feel quite privileged sitting up here. Thank you."

"My pleasure I'm sure, Madam."

After a short wait we are all making our way to The Guest House in style. I've never travelled, albeit a short journey, by horse and carriage. I, along with the others, am enjoying the experience. I love the sound made by the horses hooves, 'clip clop', 'clip clop'.

Once I'd checked in at Reception, I was escorted to my room by a lady. "Wow! The decor in here is wonderful."

"I hope your stay here will be to your satisfaction, Madam."

"Thank you, I'm sure it will."

The room is reasonably spacious for a start, there is a king size bed which looked so comfortable, and it is because I tried it. There is a small settee facing towards the window which seems to overlook the garden below. There is plenty of space to store my clothes and shoes.

Once I am settled, I make myself a cup of coffee and move over to the window to see what is outside. My room leads out on to a balcony, which overlooks the most exquisite flower garden I've ever seen. This is a garden that I could only dream of. It is, what I would consider, perfection. I would think that Lionel would have a problem achieving this for me at home. After finishing my second cup of coffee I go out into the garden for a closer look. When I was here a few weeks ago I didn't have much time to view and explore the garden.

A bit further along from the garden I discover a lake and notice that there are a few people fishing. Realising that I hadn't enough time to walk around the rest of the estate I walked back to The Guest House before getting ready for dinner. There is still some time left to explore the inside of The Guest House. I only had a quick glimpse when I was here last. Inside there is slightly less light but there's a lot of dark wooden panelling so it makes it seem darker than perhaps it truly is.

I enter through the front porch into the reception area which, as I remembered, opens into the lounge. I didn't notice last time, but this time I notice the colourful orchids in the recesses around the reception and lounge area, such a variety of pretty colours.

I noticed that there was a sign showing the way to the indoor swimming pool and spa areas. Unfortunately, I didn't know about these facilities, otherwise I would have packed my swimsuit. I'm not the strongest of swimmers but I really enjoy the exercise and it's good for me. I decide to get a drink from the bar, a medium dry white wine. Lovely. There are other residents enjoying a drink and I notice that there is a table free so I sit down, sipping my wine, while watching people coming and going. This is a real change for me. This is the life I've always been dreaming of.

Frederick comes through reception holding a clipboard and he looks rather harassed. He isn't looking for me, that is obvious. As he walks by he just happens to look my way and spots me. I wave to him and smile.

"Hi."

He makes his way over to me.

"I am sorry, my dear, that I wasn't able to greet you earlier; something unexpected happened which I've got to sort out. Can I get you another drink or anything to eat?"

"No, I'm ok right now, but thank you anyway."

"I'll meet you down here, in say, a couple of hours if that's alright. We'll have a meal here in our restaurant. I won't feel like cooking myself tonight. I'll have a word with Howard, our restaurant manager, to reserve us a table."

"Oh, that's fine with me. Lovely."

"See you later, my dear."

"Yes, take care, Frederick."

I watch him disappear. I think he somehow went out of the back door, but I can't be sure. A few minutes pass when I notice a lady carrying a glass of wine approaching my table. She smiles,

"With compliments of the management, Madam."

"Thank you. That's very kind."

"You're very welcome."

I check my watch and decide to take this glass of wine with me to my room and as I'm getting ready I take small sips from the glass until it's all gone. Delicious.

I make my way down to reception and order another glass of wine from the bar. There are a lot more people milling about in the lounge. A spare table is in short supply at the moment. So I stand waiting and admire one of the orchids. I love gardening but I wouldn't know what's involved with the care of orchids. I would think that they need a lot of care. I'll have to ask Frederick when I see him.

As I'm viewing a landscape scene hanging on the wall I can hear music coming from the drawing room.

I'm tempted to follow my ears and go in there, but I'm beginning to feel a little hungry. My stomach is starting to make some noise. I wish Frederick would come. Quite frankly I'm just beginning to get a bit fed up with waiting. I'm just going to give him a few minutes longer before I decide what to do.

"Oh Melissa, I'm so so sorry for missing you today. It's just been one of those weeks where there seems to be no end to it, just one thing after another. I'm really sorry, please forgive me. This is not what I had planned. Believe me."

"I'm glad you came when you did. I was just about to give up on you. I don't like being kept waiting, particularly in a public place by myself. It makes me feel so cheap. I'm sorry your day, your week hasn't gone to plan but I've had a reasonably nice day. Some things are often sent to try us, we just have to make the best of a bad job."

"I don't want to burden you with my troubles. I don't know about you but I could eat everything put before me. I haven't eaten anything since breakfast."

"Yes, the same here."

He took me by my hand and led me into the restaurant. Wow! I couldn't believe my eyes. What an impression. The restaurant was quite large in size but very tasteful and personal. The ceilings, apart from the beams, had halogen lighting and around the walls hung portraits and *objets d'art* which were all lit by spot lights. The ceiling and walls were red period paint. The chairs were upholstered in the same colour. The tables were round with white linen table cloths, crystal glass, silver place mats and cutlery. All the tables were lit by white candles and all had a posy of red roses in the centre. This was truly exclusive. I felt very privileged but humble at the same time.

"Frederick, this room is so beautiful. I've never dined in such luxurious surroundings before. It's so exquisite."

"Oh, glad you like it. I don't. This is my sisters' doing. They insisted that this is what our guests like apparently. They will be happy that you like it."

As soon as Howard casts eyes on Frederick he views the table plan and then very swiftly leads us down the room to our table in a corner. Howard pulls a chair out for me and once I am seated he places a napkin on my knee.

"Thank you."

"Sir, here is the menu and wine list, madam. Can I get you a drink?"

"I'll wait until I know what Frederick is going to order. Thank you."

"Very well. Sir, can I get you a drink while you peruse the menu?"

"Yes, Howard, can you bring us two bottles of our best champagne and a jug of iced water please."

"Certainly sir, I'll arrange this right away for you."

"Thank you, Howard."

"Now Melissa, once you've chosen what you'd like to order from our menu, you can tell me all about yourself. I know we've spoken several times on the phone, but personally, I prefer face to face contact."

"Yes I agree, but I need to order some food. I'm really hungry. This menu offers a good variety of food. I'll need time to decide."

"Take all the time you need, my dear. There's no rush."

"Sir, here's your champagne, and your jug of iced water will follow shortly."

"Thank you, John."

"Would you like me to serve your champagne, sir?"

"No, that's fine. I'll have that pleasure."

Frederick wrapped the towel around the top of the bottle and slowly turned the wire. Within a few seconds the cork was popped and champagne was being poured in my champagne flute.

"There you are, my dear, tell me what you think of it."

I took the glass and held it at eye level. I could see all the tiny bubbles floating to the top. The champagne was crystal clear, that's how it should be. I then sniffed it with my nose and it smelt delicious, not too dry and not too sweet. I then took a sip and sucked in a little air and swished the champagne around my mouth and then, instead of spitting it out, I swallowed it.

"That's really marvellous. It's the best I've ever tasted."

"What region is it?"

"I'm glad you like it. We make it here. It's, I suppose, our own label, we only use it here in the restaurant. We don't produce that many bottles, our land is divided between cattle, sheep and wheat. About five or so years ago a small pasture became available to us. I just told our farm manager that we should use it to experiment with.

So between us we decided to grow grapes just for the sheer hell of it. If it didn't work out then we could try something else. In our garden area we grow mostly vegetables and fruit anyway. So why not?"

"Why not, indeed?"

"That first year the grapes formed and grew, we didn't have much of a crop but it kept our staff happy and our farm shop stocked. Now we have our own, but very tiny, vineyard."

"Frederick, this all sounds really fascinating."

"You certainly know how to taste and appreciate wine, you've demonstrated that. Melissa, I know that you are a teacher, but do you have any interests in the business?"

"No, my ex-husband, Neville, ran a small restaurant in Speckleton several years ago. Not like the wine you have here, the wine tasting experience comes from that. One of our suppliers called Mark, in order to make a sale, opened a bottle and then he demonstrated this technique to us. After that Neville became a valued customer and Mark, in his own way, looked after us. At Christmas he'd give us a few bottles of champagne, free of charge, of course."

"Are you ready to order now, my dear?"

"Yes, I'm going to have a fish dish, it sounds delicious."

"So am I. Can I say, a very good choice. I don't want to sound pompous but those fish were probably caught here today from our lake."

"Oh, I saw people fishing there this afternoon but I didn't have time to explore."

"Oh, you managed to find it."

"Yes, well I stumbled upon it really. There were several paths to walk and I chose that one."

"Right, let's order. Howard, Howard we're ready to order."

Howard sent a waitress down and she takes our order. While we are in conversation the jug of iced water arrives. I pour some in a glass for me and offer the jug to Frederick while talking to him.

"Now that's enough, for the moment, about me, Frederick. How about you? I know very little about you personally."

"Well, I too was married, like you, many many years ago. My wife's name was Catherine, and not long after we were married she became pregnant, with child. We were so much looking forward to our new life together and looking so much forward to the birth of our new son or daughter. We were so happy. We'd known each other since we were children. Then one day she seemingly caught a fever and became increasingly weak. She wasn't very concerned about her own health but she did worry as to the health of our unborn baby. One day she couldn't get out of bed, she had become increasingly weaker. She wasn't eating very much either. Florry moved in with us and she cared for Catherine while I had to go to work. Florry made all kinds of broth to try and

49

encourage Catherine to eat and poultices to try and break the fever. Latterly, we called in the doctor, who tried his various pills and potions, the use of which he could not guarantee the life of our baby. Then one day I had to make a decision. The doctor believed he could save Catherine but not the baby and I had to choose because the doctor couldn't. After quite a few gruelling hours with my conscience I chose to save Catherine. It wasn't an easy decision and Catherine wasn't in any fit state to choose for herself. So in effect the baby was aborted to enable the doctor to intensify the treatment on Catherine. Unfortunately it all went horribly, horribly wrong and as a consequence Catherine's heart couldn't stand the shock of the doctor's actions. She was very weak and I lost them both. The baby did cry for a few minutes but then he died in my arms about the same time as his mother. The hardest thing for me was that I couldn't save either of them. I felt so powerless and hopelessly useless. Anyway they are both buried together and are here on the estate in the old grave yard." Frederick's tears were running down his face; he was actually reliving that terrible, terrible ordeal.

"Frederick, I'm so sorry, I didn't know, I didn't realise. You now have me crying, I'm so, so sorry."

"Let's talk about other things, shall we, but I do need you to know this, I want to be completely honest with you. I don't want us to have any secrets." Frederick is now wiping his eyes with a white handkerchief which he pulls out of his jacket pocket.

"Oh good, our food has arrived."

"This looks and smells delicious."

"Yes, the presentation is fine."

"Frederick, I've been thinking, were you and your wife living or visiting in say, Africa or India?"

"No! Why do you ask?"

"Well, about your story when losing your wife and baby. It sounds like something out of one of my history books, say from Victorian times, for example.

"Perhaps it does, but I'm telling you the truth, Melissa. Now can we talk of more pleasant things. It's not good to dwell in the past. What's happened has happened and nothing can be done to bring my wife or baby back to me. Please let's enjoy our meal and time together. Life once more is extremely precious to me now, now that I've found you, dear lady." Frederick stopped eating; he reached across the table and took hold of my hand and he kissed it very tenderly.

"Frederick, I haven't known you for very long but already I feel very comfortable around you. You really make me feel very, very valued and I haven't felt like this for a very long time. I agree about the past, but we do need to confide in each other if we are to have no secrets."

"Yes, but not tonight. This fish is so succulent and very tasty. It's wonderful."

"Yes, it is. Can I have some more champagne please? My glass is empty."

"Yes, of course, let me pour some more into your glass. There."

"Thank you. I'm really enjoying myself. Shall we drink to that?"

"Yes, why not? Let's."

After we've eaten our meal Frederick asks, "Would you like a dessert or pudding, Melissa?"

"No, but I would like to finish with a cup of coffee. Are you having a sweet?"

"No, but I too would like to have a cup of coffee before I retire for the night. We can go into The Snug and then the restaurant staff can finish off and go home. They do all work very hard and I try not to take advantage of that."

Frederick takes hold of my hand and leads me into The Snug. Apart from a couple of bar staff and us, the room is completely empty. Frederick chooses a side table and in a few minutes a coffee pot, cream and sugar are placed on our table together with beautifully decorated cups and saucers.

"Would you like anything to go with your coffee, sir?"

"No, not tonight, thanks. Melissa, would you like a brandy or whisky to accompany your coffee?"

"No, I'm fine, thanks. Coffee is just fine. Thank you."

"If you could just excuse me for a minute I need to go to the loo."

"Yes, I need one too. So see you back in here in just a few minutes."

I'm making my way back to The Lounge because I know there are some toilets in there when someone says "There are toilets in here, madam," and points to a short corridor not far from the bar.

"Thank you."

"You're welcome, madam."

After relieving myself I make my way back to our table where Frederick has just poured us a cup of coffee.

"You found them alright, then?"

"Yes, thank you, Frederick, a member of staff pointed them out to me. In all fairness I was going to The Lounge."

"Tomorrow I will meet you in The Lounge at about 11:30 a.m. providing that's alright with you. I'll take you on a tour around the farm and museum if you would like that."

"Yes, that sounds fine. Thank you."

"I won't be able to have breakfast with you in the morning because there's something I need to sort out."

"No, that's fine. Thank you. This coffee is lovely, it's just what I need."

"We could have had a latte or cappuccino if we had dined earlier. The machines and their pipes have to be washed through before the bar staff go home."

"No. This is fine. I do like latte and cappuccino but not as late as this. For me a pot of coffee makes a welcome change. I normally have instant when I'm at home."

Once I'd finish my coffee, "I'm getting really tired now; if it's alright with you I'm going to retire for the night. I've had a lovely time here today. Thank you, Frederick."

"Yes, I'm the same. I'll escort you, sweet lady, to your room."

"Yes, that will be fine. Thanks."

"Which room did they allocate you?"

"This one," as I point to the number on the key tag.

"That'll be on the second floor then."

"Yes, that's right."

"We'll take the lift up. Shall we?"

"Yes, that'll make a change for me. I normally use the stairs."

We took the lift up and Frederick escorts me to my room. I put my key in the lock and turn it. The door opens and I switch on the light.

"I'll see you in the morning, Melissa. Have a good night's sleep."

Frederick was going to kiss my hand but he changes his mind; he kisses me on my cheek instead.

"Good night, Frederick."

Once in my room, wow! On the dressing table there are a few potted Azaleas encased in white painted window boxes. There is a beautifully written card attached to one of them. It is from Frederick.

'My sweet, sweet Melissa. Sorry for not being with you earlier. With the greatest respect, Frederick.'

What a lovely surprise. I feel like a film star. I feel really special. What a nice gesture. Isn't that sweet?

After a good night's sleep I wake up to birds singing. After making a cup of tea I start to get ready for breakfast. Breakfast was being served in The Lounge area. The waitress escorted me to my table and while I was waiting for my pot of tea I perused the menu. Again there was a good selection of food including the usual full English breakfast, which I ordered.

After breakfast I wander into the garden and stroll, taking in the wonderful scenery and a bouquet of fragrances being emitted from a variety of rose bushes. I find a small enclosed garden which is delightful. There is a folly close to a fish pond so I sit down and watch the fish swimming and darting around. I keep checking my watch because I didn't want to be late and keep Frederick waiting, which, in a way, spoilt my few moments of total relaxation.

When I return to the lounge area Frederick is already waiting for me.

"Hi, Frederick. Have you been waiting here long?"

"No, I've only just got here."

"Would you like a coffee, Melissa, before our little tour?"

"No thanks, I'm ok for now, maybe later. Before we go Frederick, I would just like to thank you for the beautiful flowers in my room. They're wonderful and what a lovely gesture. Thank you."

"I'm glad you like them. You must take them home with you. They will remind you of me, sweet lady."

"I won't be able to take them all, it will be quite awkward taking them back on the train. I might be able to manage one of them. Thank you."

"Right, let's make our way to the farm."

When we arrived at the farm there were quite a lot of people looking around. We came to a row of stone cottages. Frederick escorts me into one of them. The lady of the house is wearing a Victorian costume and is demonstrating with a spinning wheel turning sheep's wool into yarn. We are free to wander and look around the cottage. It gave an insight of how people lived in those days, a living history. Interesting.

In the back yard there is a pig in a small outbuilding and hanging from a hook above, wrapped in a white muslin cloth, is the remains of a previously cured pig.

"How would we survive without fridges and freezers?"

"Like this," replied Frederick, pointing to the carcass.

There was a tin bath hanging from the cottage wall.

"How would you like to bathe in one of those, Melissa?"

"That's a bit basic for me, I'm afraid, I do like my home comforts. Although my Granny always reminisced about bath night when she was a girl, having a bath in front of a log fire with plenty of bubbles."

Frederick takes my hand and we go to the cottage next door. A lady is sitting on a stool cooking a chicken on a spit and turning the handle by hand. There is a man sitting in an armchair weaving slats into a basket. He said it took him five hours to make one basket and the basket would have been used to collect eggs or vegetables from the garden. Even today it has many uses. The smell of the chicken roasting was making me feel hungry. It did look good.

"If you're ready, Melissa, we'll make our way down to the craft centre."

"That's fine. Ok."

At the craft centre, apart from all the lovely things that are for sale, there are ladies behind the counter. One is knitting, one is working on a tapestry, one is crocheting and one is embroidering. None of which I can do.

I must have said, without realising, my comments out loud, because the lady who was crocheting replied, "Anyone can crochet, knit or sew. It's easy. If we can do it so, can you! All you need, madam, is some time. I normally crochet in the evening after work, just to unwind. It also keeps my mind active and I've created something to show for the time spent. We all donate what we make to the shop. We have a good boss who provides us with our tools and materials. Don't you, sir?" she mentioned as she looked at Frederick. Frederick blushes and seems really embarrassed. She then continued, "We run informal evenings, every now and again, anyone can come. We don't advertise but we do post information on the notice board around the reception. I can't be more specific because the damned notice board keeps being moved."

"I'll have a word with Beatrice when I get the opportunity," replied Frederick. He then turns to me and says, "Would you like anything from either the gift or craft shop, Melissa?"

"Yes, I would. I like most of the things on sale here but I have to be really practical. Everything I earn has to go on paying my bills and helping Evie with her university fees."

"If you're ready, then, we'll make our way back to The Guest House. I don't know about you, but I need to have something to eat."

"Yes, I could eat something. Although I was going to have a meal later when I get home."

"When I'm with you, Melissa, time seems to fly by. It will soon be time for you to go home, won't it?"

"Yes, I'm afraid so. Let's not think about that now. I'm enjoying myself. I really like being with you, Frederick."

"Thank you, my dear, now shall we go?"

"Yes, let's."

On our way back to The Guest House a squirrel runs across our path and in four giant leaps its climbs an old brick wall and disappears from view. It makes climbing a tall wall look completely effortless.

Frederick is so knowledgeable about the garden. He knows all the Latin names of the plants and shrubs growing there.

When we arrived at The Guest House Frederick found out that he had forgotten to reserve us a table in The Restaurant. He wasn't sure what time we needed a table so he takes me into The Drawing/Music Room and we order our food from the room service menu. There isn't much choice but we order two steak and onion sandwiches and two latte coffees.

Wow! This room is much larger than The Restaurant. It is very light, colourful and airy, but very grand. The ceiling, at some time, had been painted by an artist. The theme is a hunting scene which I don't find very appealing but the detail is exquisite. Ironically there are beautiful crystal chandeliers hanging from it. There is a very grand white marble fire surround and mantelpiece. At the other end of the room there are French doors which seem to open out onto a very large terrace.

There is a lady dressed in medieval costume sitting and playing the harpsichord. The sound it makes is divine.

There are only a few people in here. This is a great room for relaxation.

"This is a very grand room," and I can see that Frederick loves the music as much as me.

"Yes, this is my favourite room. We've had some jolly times here. I have many happy memories. We hold our Christmas and New Year staff parties here, everyone coming together and enjoying themselves."

"It must cost a lot of money to run your guest house, Frederick. I wouldn't know where to begin."

"Not really, Melissa, we are quite self-sufficient here, we grow most of what we eat. Although we do rely on our local cash n' carry for commodities such as sugar, tea, coffee, etcetera. We carry out our own maintenance and repairs. We also have a good pool of staff, all willing to work as a team and not afraid of pitching in, as and when required. We don't believe in having waste, we recycle everything."

Three waitresses arrive at our table, one with the sandwiches, one with the coffees and one bringing a tray of home-made sauces which, by the way, complement the meat beautifully. Frederick signs a docket when one

of the waitresses says, "Enjoy your food sir, madam."
We both say "Thank you" spontaneously.

"Hum, these sandwiches are really delicious,
Frederick. Thank you."

Tuesday

School Sports Day

According to the weather forecast it's going to rain
later. Great. It's our Sports day this afternoon, after
lunch. Never mind, I just need to remember to take my
brolly. I'm on lunch duty today so I need to remind the
children to change into their PE clothes after they've had
their lunch. I also need to advise them to use the toilet
although this should be imprinted on their brains, but a
gentle reminder won't do any harm. I'm taking my
jogging suit, T shirt, and plimsolls with me and, like the
children, will be changing at school. I'll be more
comfortable.

Everything has gone remarkably smoothly this
morning. Now the children are eating their lunch. Janice
welcomes Henry Walter, Nigel and Linda Jack. As Nigel
passes by me he asks for a jar of my special jam.
Apparently Frances took the remains of my jam to work
so Nigel could have a taste.

Henry will be presenting a cup and Nigel will be
presenting a trophy to the best sports kid. Linda will be
presenting ice cream vouchers to the children who come
1st, 2nd and 3rd. We've invited a couple of ice cream
vendors to come along. It gives the children an added
incentive to do well. When the weather is good ice
cream can be very refreshing and so satisfying.

As the morning goes on there seem to be more clouds. I wouldn't be at all surprised if it doesn't rain. Now that will spoil things so I'm keeping my fingers crossed. I try not to take the weather forecast too seriously but rain is forecast although not until later on. As I'm on lunch duty today I'll be eating with the children. I've already made the announcements so hopefully everything will continue to run smoothly. Fingers crossed.

Right, that's lunch nearly over, most of the children are now doing what they should. Wonderful. I'm just finishing my coffee when Janice comes in.

"Can you lock up the school and make sure everything is safe before you go to the sports field, please?"

"Yes, of course I can. Is everything alright?"

"No, Mum's not feeling very well. She says she's feeling dizzy."

"Oh, I'm really sorry, Janice, to hear that, but you'd better go home."

"Yes, I just needed to pick up my things. Don't forget to take the first aid kit just in case anyone gets hurt. Oh, by the way don't worry about being delayed, I've told Bernie and Phoebe to get things organised until you can take charge of sports day and the children in my absence. I've told them that you will be locking up. I'd better get going. Take care, I'll give you a ring later."

"Yes, alright. You take care. Bye."

While Bernie and Phoebe were organising the children I made a start locking up. Most of the classrooms were left just the way they should be which makes locking up quite straightforward.

As I'm walking by the Community Centre I notice the date plaque when the first centre was built. From the date engraved on it, it was over one hundred and fifty years ago. That can't be right because Frederick mentioned that he had played on the sports field as a young boy.

When I arrive on the sports field Bernie and Phoebe are organising and setting up for the first race. Henry is checking out his starter pistol, while Nigel and Linda are walking down to the finish line holding hands. The ice cream vendors are just arriving and Nigel sets about advising them where to park. Proud parents, family friends and grandparents line all along both sides of the marked racing lanes. It is quite a turn out, all things considered, including those low dark clouds.

"Please don't let it rain just yet," I say, looking up at them.

"Hi Melissa, here's your clipboard," Bernie says as he hands it to me. There are several lists of the following races and the children's names who are running. So I check off the names by calling them out and lining up the children ready to go. Phoebe is overseeing my actions, while Bernie is piling up the sacks ready for the fun races. We usually have the children doing a sack race for each year group and an egg and spoon race using small rubber balls, which balance on a tablespoon.

Henry starts off the first race and sports day is well on the way.

Once I'd got all the children lined up Phoebe took over.

"Here you are, Melissa, how did locking up go?" It was Janice.

"Hello, Janice, locking up went ok, thank you. How's your Mum?"

"She's alright now, she's got a bad bout of indigestion. I've given her a good measure of medicine."

"Here are the school keys, Janice, you'd better have them while I'm thinking about them."

"Cheers, Melissa, and thank you for your assistance. It's well appreciated."

"You're welcome, Janice."

"It looks like everything is going tickety-boo here. I'll just go and check on the others."

"Alright, Janice, I'll stay here. Just in case Phoebe or Bernie need me."

When the children have finished their races the parents and grandparents are encouraged to have a race just for the sheer fun of it.

Saturday

Mother and Evie are coming today for the weekend and Poppy came and helped me with the cleaning before they arrived.

Tonight it's Charles' 30th birthday and he's having a party on the Estate. I see a big difference in my mother. She's much happier, content, less critical, and more confident.

Evie is just finishing her coffee when Charles takes her away, presumably to the Estate. Mother and I notice that she's taking her clothes for tonight with her.

"She's obviously gone for the day," Mother observes, and I agree.

After lunch Frederick sends two of his employees, May and June, they are twins, but they are not identical. May will be giving us a massage, but as Evie has already gone out with Charles, Mother and I have a much welcomed full body massage. Lovely. June will be giving us a facial, make-up and a manicure. Mother and I feel marvellous. May and June are extremely nice.

Mother and Evie have bought me a sparkly turquoise cocktail dress to wear, which is totally different to what I normally wear. Once I've been pampered I will try it on just to see how it fits and looks. I will decide myself whether I wear it or not.

Janice will be taking her mum, Beryl, me and my mother plus Bernie and Phoebe, in her car to and from the Estate.

When May and June have left, Mother and I try on our new outfits.

"Oh, Melissa, that dress does suit you. The colour is so perfect."

"Mother, you look wonderful, too."

"Well, thank you, dear. I wasn't too sure when I tried it on in the shop, but Evie chose it, and she said it looked nice. She chose yours too."

We have a few drinks before we go, a bit of Dutch courage so to speak. I do know Nigel and Linda Jack,

Charles' mother and father, Charles, Ben and Iris. I've yet to meet the rest of the Jack family. In a way I am looking forward to going. I just hope Mother is on her best behaviour.

Janice arrives and before we know it we are travelling down to the Jacks' Estate.

Janice drops us off at the bottom of the front steps and then goes off to park her car. We go up the steps and enter through the front door which leads into a large reception area. Kim, landlady of The Kissing Gate, is on cloak room duty taking our coats and hands us all a raffle ticket in exchange for our coats. She hangs our coats on what looks like a temporary rail.

"There are a lot of coats, aren't there, Kim?" I mention.

"Yes, and you're not the last either. We're expecting in the region of three hundred guests tonight."

"Three hundred! I thought this was Charles' birthday. I didn't realise that he knew so many people. He's obviously very popular."

"Yes, Charles is a very popular man, but some of the guests here tonight are business colleagues of Henry Walters. He's showcasing his new business venture with Nigel and Linda Jack. They're hoping to use some of the rooms here for various functions. Charles' birthday is being held in the main hall this evening, just follow the other guests if you don't know the way. Frances will show you to your table. By the way, Melissa, you do look nice."

"Yes, she does," added Mother.

"Thank you, Kim, you look nice too."

"Thank you, Melissa, that's very kind of you."

As we follow the other guests Mother asks, "Who was that?"

"Mother, that was Kim, she's the landlady of The Kissing Gate pub, she's obviously helping the Jacks tonight."

When we arrive in the main hall we wait patiently for Frances because she is already showing other guests to their tables. Music is being played and the sound level is just right. I can hear some of the other guests' conversations while we are waiting.

"This is a much larger and grander do than I expected," I remarked to Mother.

"Evie did mention that Mr and Mrs Jack, to the disapproval of Charles, had gone to town with the planning of his party. Mrs Jack mentioned to Evie that they hadn't had a good party for a few years and she likes a good party. Even though it's Charles' birthday he's had very little to do with it. This isn't really what Charles wanted."

"Oh, Evie didn't say anything like that to me. By the way, it's not Mr and Mrs Jack, it's Nigel and Linda."

"I know dear, but I don't know them, so I prefer to call them Mr and Mrs Jack. Don't forget dear, I've never met them."

"Good evening, Melissa, is this your mother?" It was Frances.

"Hello, Frances, yes this is my mother. Mother, this is Frances, she's my next door neighbour."

"I'm so pleased to meet you, Frances." Mother shakes her hand.

"Let me take you all to your table, just follow me."

I look behind me and Janice has just joined us.

Once we're seated, a young girl in uniform comes to our table.

"Would you like to order your drinks, ladies and gentleman? Tonight it is a free bar! Mr and Mrs Jack have instructed us to order and fetch your drinks in order to avoid a stampede."

"A stampede!" Bernie objects.

"Yes that's what Mr and Mrs Jack want to avoid happening."

"I've never heard anything so stupid," Bernie continues.

"Bernie, just shut your mouth and order a drink," Phoebe advises.

Bernie and Phoebe both order a beer, Janice and her mum both order gin and tonic.

Mother orders a sweet sparkling white wine and I order the same.

Our table is set for ten people so there are four more guests to join us.

"I wonder who is going to join us?" Mother asks.

Janice replies, "Trisha and Harry, they will be joining us later, I think Frances and Brendan will also be joining us when they have finished their duties."

I turn to Mother and say, "I was rather hoping that Evie and Charles would be joining us."

"No, Evie told me that she and Charles will be joining the Jack family."

"Oh, great," I replied.

"The table decorations are nice, aren't they?" comments Mother.

"Yes, they are. Are those candles real?" I ask.

"No, they're battery operated," answers Janice.

"Yes, they sell them in the farm shop," Beryl, Janice's mother adds.

"Changing the subject, they use this room for functions now, you know, and Mr Walter hires his staff out to do the catering, any opportunity to make more money, eh," advised Brendan.

"I'd say," replied Bernie.

There is a fanfare and the Jack family make quite an entrance. Nigel and Linda Jack hand in hand, followed by Flight Lieutenant Steel, Lorna and Eamon, Belinda and Owen, Ben and Iris, Charles and Evie, Harvey and Toni, Henry Walter and George. As they make their way to their table Evie looks around the room, and when she spots us she waves and smiles at Mother and me.

"You know, Mother, I'm so proud of our little girl."

"Yes, so am I, but Melissa, she's no longer a little girl. She's a beautiful, confident, young lady."

"Yes, I know that, but she's still my little girl."

"Ladies and gentlemen, the carvery is now ready to serve, so if you want to get into an orderly queue. There's beef, lamb, chicken, pork, gammon and a variety of game along with a good selection of fresh vegetables and salad. The waiting staff will be around in a minute with a choice of red or white wine, whichever takes your fancy," Nigel announces.

"Good job we're not vegetarians or vegans. Eh!" remarks Brendan.

"Are you lot coming?" asks Bernie.

"I'm going to wait until the queue dissipates. What kind of wine would you prefer? Just in case the waiting staff come here before you get back," I reply.

"You carry on Bernie, me and Mum will join Melissa and Nancy in the queue later," commented Janice.

"Ok, Melissa, I'll have another beer. Is anyone else coming? Phoebe, are you coming?"

"Alright, sweetie, I'll be right behind you. Melissa, I'll have another bottle of beer too. Thanks."

"Yes, ok."

Trisha and Harry were also in no hurry to join the queue; they were sitting next to Janice and Beryl. Brendan and Frances were still deciding what they were going to do.

"I don't know about you, Frances, but I'm going to join the queue. My stomach's ready to receive something, I haven't had anything to eat since breakfast. Are you coming, love?"

"No, I'm not that hungry at the moment. I think I'll wait for the drinks to come. Are you sticking with the same to drink or are you going to have something else?"

"I'll have another beer as well. Ta."

"Melissa, Evie's looking very radiant tonight," remarks Janice.

"Yes, she is. She's very happy. Just look at her," follows Mother.

"Mother's just taken the words right out of my mouth."

Janice smiles.

I watch Evie from time to time and notice she and Charles are smiling. I also notice Charles whispering in Evie's ear, then Evie whispers in Charles' ear. They are both smiling and sniggering. They are a very loving couple and I'm slowly realising that Mother's right, she's not a little girl any more.

"Mother, shall we go and join the queue for some food?"

"Can we wait a while? Our drinks haven't come yet."

"Yes, if you like, a few more minutes won't hurt."

The drinks eventually arrive and the others return to the table with food on their plates heaped up, especially the men.

"Where are you going to put all that?" Janice remarks directed at Brendan.

"Oh, I'll find space in my belly. Believe me!"

"His stomach's like a bottomless pit, he eats loads. On a Sunday he'll eat a delicious roast then he'll follow it with a packet of biscuits or a whole tub of ice cream, if there's any in the freezer. Shopping can be a nightmare sometimes. Thank goodness for the farm shop," Frances advises.

"Frances does a lovely roast but she doesn't do puddings, so I fill up with whatever's available. Biscuits, ice cream, occasionally bags of crisps. Can you blame me? I'm used to having loads of food, me."

"You're lucky Brendan. I only have to look at something that I enjoy and then I can feel the pounds just piling on. So I have to take care with what I eat," advised Janice.

"Yes, I try to eat healthily and sensibly. I certainly think about what I'm eating," I offered.

"As do we," said Harry with Trisha agreeing by nodding her head.

"I have to say in view of all your comments the food on those plates looks really yummy," remarked Beryl.

"Yes, I agree with you, Beryl, the food does look delicious," Mother being agreeable.

"Mother, are you now ready to get in line to the carvery?" I ask.

"Yes, dear, I could eat a bit of something. Are you joining us, Beryl?"

"Yes I'm just about getting there. Are you coming Janice?"

"Yes, I'm about the same. Ladies, let's go. Are you two coming?"

"If you don't mind, Janice, we'll wait a bit longer. We're not quite ready to go as yet. I think we'll have some more to drink."

"Are you two feeling alright? You seem much quieter than usual."

"Yes, Janice, we're fine. We're not aware of being any different, really."

"Are you sure?"

"Janice, just go and get your own food. Don't worry about us. We'll sort our own food out later. Please, don't fuss. We're fine."

Janice comes and joins me, Mother and Beryl in the now very short queue.

"It looks like most of the guests are now sorted. Doesn't it?" I observed.

"There's still loads of delicious food. What a lovely spread. Everything still looks so very fresh," Mother added.

"I don't know what's up with Harry and Trisha, I've never seen them like this before. They usually enjoy themselves. Something's just not quite right," remarks Janice.

"Yes, I know, it hasn't gone without us noticing, has it, Mother?"

Mother just purses her lips and then looks at Beryl and says, "Look, I've come here tonight to really enjoy myself and if they want to be antisocial, then let them. Personally, I'm not getting involved, life's too short, they're not my friends, I hardly know them. They won't stop me from having a nice time."

Beryl replies, "Yes, Nancy, I agree with you. When you get to our age the last thing you want to see at a party is someone clearly not enjoying themselves. It can bring us down if we let it. Can't it?"

Mother nods.

One by one we all choose from the carvery and make our way back to the table. Harry and Trisha are no longer at the table. We all must have noticed but no one comments about it.

"Hey, you lot, I've ordered us five jugs of Sangria from the bar, they should be here soon. I thought we all needed cheering up. Our conversations are a bit stilted so a bit of Sangria should hit the spot. It'll get us in the party mood," Brendan advised.

"Sangria will be lovely, Brendan. Thank you," followed Janice.

"I haven't had Sangria in years. That's a nice touch. Well done, lad," compliments Mother.

The rest of us smile and nod our heads in agreement.

Flight Lieutenant Steel comes over to our table and asks Janice, "Would you like to dance?"

Janice says, "Yes."

Just as Janice is being escorted back to the table, Henry Walters approaches Janice and he leads her back on to the dance floor.

I'm so pleased for Janice. I know she's a little sweet on Henry Walters, and it's quite obvious to me now that he feels the same.

Evie comes over to Mother and me because she wants us to meet the rest of Charles' family. We all saunter over to where the Jack family are seated.

"Mum and Nan, I want you to meet Charles' sister, Belinda."

"Hello, how are you?" Belinda asks.

"We're fine. Thank you."

"I'd like you both to meet my husband, Owen," Belinda said.

"Hello, nice to meet you."

"Likewise," Owen replies.

Evie escorts us to the other side of the table. "Mum, I want you to meet Harvey."

"Hello, Harvey, it's so nice to meet you."

"Hi, it's good to meet you. I like your dress, very sexy!" Harvey must have sucked on one of the helium balloons because his voice is very highly pitched and squeaky.

"Why, thank you. It's nice of you to mention it," I say, without looking too embarrassed and trying very hard not to laugh.

"Forgive him! He's so cheeky. Hello, I'm Toni, Harvey's girlfriend."

"Hello, Toni, nice to meet you too. Don't worry about me, I can take it."

"Well, Mum, now you've met the rest of the Jack family. Mum, that dress you're wearing looks really great on you. I love that colour."

"Thank you, sweetheart. Your Nan hasn't yet met Nigel, Linda, Ben and Iris, perhaps you could introduce them to her and bring her back to our table when you've finished."

"Of course I can, Mum."

I notice Evie's left hand is bearing what looks to me to be an engagement ring. I take her hand and can't stop myself from saying, "When did you get engaged then?"

"Honestly, Mum, I didn't know anything about this. Nigel will be announcing our engagement a bit later. They didn't know either. Charles took me to the jeweller this morning and we collected the ring this afternoon. When Charles put it on my finger I didn't have the heart to take it off and put it back in the box."

"I'm glad I noticed your finger, then. It would have been a bit of a shock for me and your nan to have heard it being announced."

"I'm really sorry, Mum, I should have told you earlier but I'm so excited."

"Yes, I can see you are, sweetheart. Congratulations."

"Oh. Thank you, Mum."

"My little girl is growing up. I hope you have a longer engagement. You haven't known Charles for long. Are you sure you know what you're doing?"

"I hope so. I am old enough."

I go back to the table where Mother and I are sitting. The others are all now on the dance floor having a good time, including Beryl, who is dancing with Flight Lieutenant Steel.

It isn't long before Mother joins me at our table.

"Charles' family seem to be nice, Melissa, don't they?"

"Yes, they are."

The music stops and everyone returns to their tables.

Nigel announces, "Ladies and gentlemen, thank you for coming tonight to celebrate Charles' 30th birthday. Linda and I hope that you are enjoying yourselves. There's just one more thing that I need to announce and I hope that Charles will forgive me, but Charles and Evie got engaged today. So, everyone, if you would like to raise your glasses and join us in congratulating them on this occasion. Ladies and gentlemen; Charles and Evie."

Everyone raises their glasses and repeats "Charles and Evie."

Someone starts singing "For he's a jolly good fellow" and everyone joins in. It ends with "Hip hip hurray."

When everyone has settled down, the music commences, and some of the guests get up and start to dance.

Sunday

"Mother, I'm really looking forward to Frederick coming today. I do hope you like him, he's not a bit like Neville."

"You obviously think a lot of him, sweetheart, I'm so happy for you. Now you need to get yourself ready, he'll be here soon, I wouldn't wonder."

"Yes, look at the time, just lately time seems to fly."

"I'll sort out the breakfast pots and just tidy up a little. Has Evie got up yet?"

"Yes, Evie's already gone with Charles. She's having breakfast with the Jack family."

"She seems to be really smitten with Charles, you know."

"Yes, I'm gathering that more from her actions. I would really like to have some time to just have a decent conversation with her."

"You need to get yourself dressed."

"Yes, I'm going."

The doorbell rings and Mother goes to the door. It's Frederick.

"Oh hello, you must be Melissa's mother. I'm Frederick, where's Melissa?"

"Pleased to meet you, Frederick, Melissa's told me lots about you."

"Good, I hope."

"Yes, Melissa's getting ready, come in. Would you like a coffee, Frederick, while you wait?"

"Not at the moment, but thank you. Could you leave the door open, my chauffeur is bringing in our lunch. I told Melissa that I'd be treating you all to lunch, I just hope you won't be too disappointed with it. I bet you thought you were going out for it."

"No, not at all, Frederick. I try to keep an open mind in such matters."

The chauffeur brings in several stainless steel containers and stacks them on one of my work tops.

"Thank you, James. Will you be able to manage the box of wine?"

"Yes, sir, I'll be fine. Thank you."

"Hello, Melissa, my dear, you look really radiant. Would you like a glass of wine?"

"No, it's a bit early for me but please pour one for yourself. Mother, would you like to try a glass of wine? It's really delicious."

"I'll open a bottle of my champagne for you to try. Can I call you Mother?"

"My name is Nancy, actually."

"Alright, Nancy."

"Here you are, Frederick," I say, handing over two champagne flutes.

"Thank you, my dear. Here you are, Nancy, tell me what you think of this."

"Thank you, Frederick, that looks nice and refreshing."

Mother looks at the bubbles in the flute and with two gulps she'd drunk the lot.

"Oh, that's really nice. It has a really nice flavour. Can I have a look at the label, please, Frederick?"

"Yes, you can, Nancy, but it won't help you. We now make this at The Mound and you won't be able to buy this anywhere."

"What, you mean you grow the grapes here in the UK?"

"Yes, we acquired a pasture about five years ago, and this is what we now produce."

"If you want any customers I can provide you with a list."

"I'm afraid we don't produce enough to supply anyone, only for our guests. I thought I'd give you both a little treat."

"I hope you don't think me rude, but can I have another glass, please?"

"Certainly, just help yourself. I've brought plenty with me. I'll just put the others in the fridge for later. That one's been cooling on the way over in my limo."

"If you could both just excuse me, Mother, Frederick, for a moment, I've just got to go outside. Moggie's bringing home a souvenir. Make yourselves comfortable."

Moggie is making her way up to the back door dragging what very much looks like a squirrel; it is either injured or dead. When Moggie sees me she walks towards me and she drops it by my feet. She looks so proud as if to say look what I've got. My heart goes out to that poor animal, it certainly isn't moving; it looks dead to me. Not wanting to upset Moggie I stroke her several times, she is purring very positively and loudly and is wrapping herself around my legs. I pick up the poor creature and try to decide what to do with it. I can't bury it because I am wearing my best clothes and Mother and Frederick are waiting for me to return. So I decide to put it in the garden shed and close the shed door to prevent Moggie from playing with it. When I return I wash my hands in the kitchen sink. Moggie must have decided to stay outside in the garden because she didn't follow me in.

I can hear Mother giggling with Frederick in my conservatory. I think she's a bit squiffy. She must like Frederick because she's giggling. I have noticed over this weekend that Mother seems to be much happier than I've ever seen her, my special jam must be working.

"You two seem to be getting on, are you both alright?"

"Yes, Frederick is just telling me that his family used to live in this village and, would you believe they used to live in a cottage which was built on this site?"

"Yes, Frederick mentioned it to me some time ago. Mother, you know that twisted tree in the orchard, well Frederick has a few in his garden."

"Oh, I have to say personally I don't like it. Just looking at it gives me the creeps, but your special jam, Melissa, is divine. So you shouldn't judge something on appearances alone."

"Yes, Mother, I know what you mean, but I find it fascinating. I've taken several photographs of it through the seasons, at sunrise and sunset. I was sure that you'd already seen them."

"Yes, I have, but honestly I don't share your fascination."

"Melissa, I'll need to warm through our lunch and I think it's time to switch your conventional oven to the correct temperature. Can you come and assist me, please? Nancy, before we go, can I get you another champagne, tea or coffee?

"Look if I'm honest, yes you could! But I've got to be sensible, so no thank you, Frederick, but thank you for asking."

When Frederick comes through to the kitchen I've already sorted the oven and am getting my best blue willow pattern dinner set ready for the food.

"Frederick, will you need these dishes for the food or are you going to serve the food directly onto the plates?"

"I'll serve the food directly onto the plates. Let's save on washing up. You can leave them here, I'll warm them up."

"It doesn't matter to me, Frederick, whichever way you choose, because I do have a small dishwasher so it doesn't make that much difference to me."

"Oh, I do hope these catering tins fit into your oven. I've only just realised."

"They won't all fit in at once obviously because you've brought a lot with you. It must be some kind of feast but you will be able to rotate them. There are two shelves already in the oven but if you need a third I can bring it out from storage."

"No, that won't be necessary, what you have already will be fine. I've brought enough for four because I thought Evie would be joining us for lunch."

"Nowadays when she visits I don't know if she's staying in or going out. Charles came earlier and he's taken her to join his family. Now, I'm just going to set the table. Are you alright, Mother, you've gone quiet?" I crept into the conservatory and Mother had dropped off to sleep. That's the champagne. It's really nice to see her relaxed.

"Is Nancy alright?"

"Yes, she's asleep," I whisper, as I'm passing by Frederick on my way to the dining table.

Everything apart from the plates is already on the table. I did it earlier before getting dressed. It's not as posh as The Guest House but it's cosy and less formal. I love my home.

I return to the kitchen. "Is there anything that I can help you with, Frederick?"

"No, everything is under control here. Do you think I could see your photographs of your Tinsel tree, please, Melissa?"

"Yes, you can have a look at them this afternoon, after we've had lunch, if you like."

"Yes, that's fine. You see I'm very interested and fascinated with it, too. Could I perhaps have a jar of your special jam, please, Melissa?"

"Yes, you can, but your jam is supremely better. Hum, whatever you've got in those tins. it smells scrumptious."

"I've only brought a main and pudding, I don't bother nowadays with a starter. There's roast pheasant with a forcemeat stuffing and a port wine jus and assorted roast root vegetables. For afters there's a choice of Elizabethan syllabub or sticky toffee pudding with home-made vanilla custard."

"Hum, that sounds good."

"Yes, it does. It's a long time since I've had pheasant," added Mother.

"Yes, same here, Mother, it will make a change. If you want, Mother, would you like to come through and get seated before Frederick serves the food?"

"Yes, I'm just getting out of my chair."

"Melissa, will you serve the rest of the champagne, please?"

"Yes, I most certainly will. I've been looking forward to having a glass for ages. Do you want any help, Mother, getting to the table?"

"No, thank you, dear, I can manage, the champagne its now losing its grip on me. Thank you."

After a delicious meal and polite conversation between the three of us, Frederick views the photographs of my Tinsel tree. I take Frederick first on a tour around the inside of my cottage, then around the flower garden at the front, the vegetable patch at the side, ending in the orchard by the Tinsel tree at the back.

"You know, this Tinsel tree here has been around for a long time. It was here when my family lived here. My mother used to make jam from its fruit. I don't know where our cottage was situated when we lived here, I was only a small boy, so I don't remember, but my father would know. You see my father worked as a farm labourer and the cottage was tied into his work. He used to work for a land owner named Uriah Jack."

"I wonder if it's the same family on the Estate down the lane."

"I think that's more than likely. Landowners usually stay put."

"In fact, Evie is now engaged to Charles, Nigel and Linda's son."

"Anyway, one day all the family gathered around the tree to give praises to the tree because it was the only tree in the orchard to produce an abundant crop of fruit.

Giving praises to the land, singing around trees, etcetera, wasn't unusual within our family and the time we lived in. We always said grace at the table, so why not directly to the trees. Anyway our neighbours witnessed this event and reported what they saw to the village elders. They decided to give us a warning and we were strongly advised to leave this village."

I clearly wasn't on the same wavelength as Frederick; had I missed an important part of what he was saying? The action seemed a bit drastic, didn't it?

"Frederick, I'm not really truly understanding what you've just said. It seems a tad drastic, doesn't it?"

"Melissa, to you, yes, probably." He moves closer to me and places his hands on my arms and looks directly into my eyes. "You see, Melissa, my family and I come from a different time."

"A different time, what are you talking about? Are you some kind of time traveller? I've seen similar, albeit fictitious, on the television and in books, but I've never really believed that any one, or indeed an entire family could possibly exist from the past. No, this can't be possible."

"Melissa, just listen to me, please, there are things about me you need to know. I want to be completely

84

honest with you. Personally, I believe that we're meant to be together, or could it be just coincidence that you found me at The Mound? Or could it be this tree? Perhaps it possesses magical powers!"

"Frederick, please, let me go, you are scaring me. I need to go back to my mother, just to see if she's alright. I'm feeling cold. I need my cardigan."

"Alright, Melissa, but there's so much more I need to tell you. Can we continue this conversation a bit later?"

"If you like."

I left Frederick in the orchard. I am so confused I don't know what to believe any more. He seems genuine enough, but to believe that he's from a different time. I need some time to absorb all this."

"Mother, are you alright?"

"Yes, I'm ok. I could see you and Frederick in the garden so I've tidied up. I've washed some of Frederick's tins but I don't know if you realise but there's more food in the others. You will need to transfer this into some airtight containers and put them in the fridge."

"Oh, I didn't know that there was any more food, Frederick didn't say. What is there? Let's sort this out now, shall we?"

There is some cheese, slices of pork pie and some cold cuts. There are some portions of cake, home-made scones and pastries.

"Would you like to take some food back with you, Mother? There's way too much just for me."

"Yes, that would be nice. I'm having some friends over and this food will save me from doing some baking. This food will certainly impress them."

"Yes, just help yourself, Mother. Take what you need."

"Lovely. Thank you."

"I'm just going to find Frederick. I'm going to take him on a walk around the village. We won't be long."

I go into the garden, and as I'm walking by my garden shed I notice that the padlock is open and when I open the door the squirrel is not in there. I wonder where it is. I carry on making my way around the back when I see Frederick. It looks as though he's putting the squirrel on the wall. The squirrel sits very still for a few moments and when Frederick takes a few steps back the squirrel disappears over the wall.

"Hi, Frederick, I wonder if you'd like to go for a walk around the village."

"Yes, that would be nice. I just need to wash my hands before we do, if you don't mind."

"No, that's fine. Oh thank you for the food, that's a lovely gesture. I really appreciate it. Thank you."

"Oh, I'm sorry, I forgot all about that, I meant to sort it out after lunch. I brought it for our tea, if that's not too presumptuous of me."

"No, not at all. Mother and I have it sorted."

Once Frederick has washed his hands we make our way down to the Community Centre.

On the way we see Harry playing football in the garden with his three boys. He smiles and waves to us as we go by.

"As I've mentioned to you before, when I was a small boy I and my two sisters, Florry and Beatrice, used to play on that field and here at the kissing gate I've kissed a few girls too."

Frederick draws me close and kisses me on the cheek. "There, now you've been kissed at the kissing gate. Although this is a newer version than we had," he says, as he touched the gate.

I place my hand on his and give it a gentle squeeze. Frederick reciprocates with a smile.

"Frederick, I wish I'd got more time to show you more of the village but looking at the time I need to get back home, because Mother and Evie will be leaving soon and I would like to see them before they go. I haven't seen very much of Evie."

"Of course you do, but we do need to talk before I go."

"Yes I know, but I can't talk about that now."

We make our way back to my cottage. Just as we turn the corner from Main Street we see Frances with Katie and Justin. It looks like they are going to take Molly for a walk down the lane.

Mother is just finishing her cup of tea when I arrive home.

"I've not long made a pot of tea if you both would like a cup."

"Yes, Mother, that would be very welcome. Frederick, would like you like a cup?"

"Yes, that would be nice."

"The taxi will be coming soon."

"Yes, I know. Has Evie come back yet?"

"No, but you know what she's like."

"Yes, only too well, although just lately she comes back about five minutes before the taxi arrives."

Frederick, Mother and I make polite conversation in my sitting room. I have a good view of my driveway so can see when Evie returns. Mother is all ready to go, she's just passing time, she and Evie won't be able to have tea with Frederick and me, there isn't much time.

The taxi arrives but there's no sign of Evie. Frederick and I help Mother with her things and walk with her up my driveway.

"Frederick, it was really nice to meet you and thank you very much for lunch, it really was delicious," Mother says, as she shakes Frederick's hand.

"Nice to have finally met you, Nancy, have a safe journey back."

"Mother, will you be alright to travel on your own?"

"Yes, sweetheart, I'll be fine, I think."

"Can you ring me when you get back, please?"

"Yes, of course I can. Don't worry, I'll be alright."

"Ok, have a safe journey, Mother. Take care. Bye, bye."

After the taxi has gone Frederick and I return to my cottage.

"Melissa, do you fancy something to eat? It is nearly tea time."

"I won't want too much, just a nibble, perhaps a slice of cake."

I don't know where Frederick puts his food but he certainly enjoys it. I haven't forgotten my lunch. I certainly haven't worked off the calories today. I don't want to gain any weight. I truly believe in input/output. It looks like Frederick is one lucky devil who can eat anything he likes or desires without gaining an ounce. Me, it feels as though I only have to look at something really delicious and I can feel those pounds pile on, quite literally. It might be that Frederick is working all of the time, at least he has the opportunity to work outside in the fresh air, whereas for me I'm cooped up inside while I'm at work.

"Are you alright, sweetheart, you're awfully quiet. Your complexion has gone very pale."

"I'll be alright, Frederick. I just need some time to think. A lot's happened over this weekend, I just need time to adjust and I need to get a good night's sleep."

"I do understand, Melissa, but please don't shut me out."

"No, it probably looks like that to you, Frederick, but I'm really not. Which piece of cake would you like?"

"I'm going to have a sandwich, have you got any bread, please?"

"Yes there's some in the bread bin, and if you want some spread there's some in the fridge."

"Don't you have any butter?"

"No, I use spread not butter. If you put your food on this tray we can watch television."

"No, I would prefer to sit at the table and converse with you."

"Yes, that'll be nice."

"Melissa, I need you to listen to me, I'm not a time traveller, but I and my family have existed for a very long time. You see, it all started with that Tinsel tree. My mother, Martha, like you, started to make jam because food was very scarce. Our landlord rationed our food and there was only enough food to barely keep us alive. We were only allowed a small percentage of the fruit that we grew in the orchard, but the Tinsel tree fruit wasn't included. Back then the jam that my mother made wasn't like the jam that is made now. As children, to my parents' dismay, we didn't like the look of the Tinsel tree jam nor the fruit. When we eventually settled at The Mound my father, Rowan, discovered an orchard which included another Tinsel tree. So my mother was able to continue making jam and with an abundance of fruit she started to make wine. One day, when my father was pruning one of the Tinsel trees, he found what he thought was leaking sap from it. Curiosity got the better of him so he touched it with his finger and found it to be sticky. He decided to lick his finger and, quite surprisingly, he found it had a slightly sweet palatable taste. After a short period of time he drove a piece of wood into the trunk of that tree and hung a small pot from it. A small amount of sap drained from it and he took it to show my mother. She, unlike my father, was a bit more reluctant to try it. She was a bit more cautious than my father. He told her that he had tried it a few days before and he was still alive! Eventually she tried it, liked it, and told my father that he could try it on his porridge, before allowing we children to consume it. As time passed and as sugar became more refined the quality of the jam seemed more appealing to us children. Each year my father was able to grow other Tinsel trees and my mother continued to make jam and wine. Eventually we were all consuming the jam and the syrup."

"Where's all this going? Yes, don't forget I'm consuming your jam now!"

"Well, we've latterly found out that when the jam is consumed over a period of some time and provided it is used on a regular basis, our Tinsel tree jam has some healing properties."

"Wow. Tell me more."

"Well, we know it can reduce anxiety, depression, blood pressure, and cholesterol. It can also increase a sense of wellbeing in some people. One side effect, however, which may be a result of consuming our jam, is gaining an extrasensory skill or skills. These can manifest themselves in so many ways, but it affects people in different ways. It's very much down to the individual and can depend on lots of different variables."

"You now keep mentioning people. I thought your family, guests and I are the only ones that were having your jam."

"Yes, that is correct, sweetheart. Would you like some more wine?"

"Yes, please."

CHAPTER V

Friday tea time

The telephone rings. I answer, it's Mother.

"Hello dear, I've received a letter from Neville."

Neville is my ex partner and Evie's father. Guess what? He wants to see me after how many years!

"Melissa, are you there? Speak to me, dear. Look, I know it's a bit of a shock. It was to me receiving this letter. Melissa, darling, speak to me."

I was shocked but all I could think of was Evie.

"Mother, yes it's a bit of shock but what about Evie? Did you say anything to her?"

"No! Melissa, I haven't told Evie. Neville wants to see you. He wants me to give you his mobile number. Evie doesn't need to know. Does she?"

"No, that's right she doesn't."

Mother gives me his contact details.

"Mother, this is a bit of shock and if you don't mind I'm going to end this call. I'm really sorry but I don't know what to say. I'll have to give this some thought.

I'll get in touch with you perhaps in a few days. Take care, Mother."

"Yes I do understand, dear. You take care."

"Yes alright, Mother. Bye."

"Yes, bye bye dear."

I wonder why he wants to see me after all this time. It must be at least eighteen years since he left us.

After several mugs of coffee and many circuits around my garden I decide to contact Neville and we arrange to meet in Tinville city centre at a cafe/bar which he often frequents apparently, tomorrow. To be truthful, I've not taken that much interest in the city centre since graduating from Tinville University. Any way Neville has given me explicit directions to where I need to be.

I'm not really sure that I'd be able to recognise him after all these years. It's been a long time. I'm not sure if I'll get much sleep either.

I get out of bed, I get ready, and reluctantly board the train to Tinville.

I haven't dressed up, in fact, quite the opposite. After trying on several clothes options I decided to dress comfortably, jogging suit, trainers and my very large black shoulder bag.

I arrive at the cafe/bar and I can't see Neville, so I decide to get a coffee and sit on one of the window stools. From here I can see who comes in and who goes out, also there are good views both up and down the shopping mall. So I could possibly see Neville.

I must be nervous inside because I get this very strong urge to visit the Ladies. If I'm truthful, I really don't want to be here. I return to the stool where I'd been sitting when I hear someone shouting my name. This must be Neville.

"Hi, Melissa, I thought it was you. You're looking good. In fact you're looking fucking good."

I wince; I'm not that keen on anyone using the 'f' word, particularly when it's directed at me.

"I suppose you're Neville," I said sarcastically.

"Don't you recognise me?"

"No! Not instantly! Are you here with your friends?"

"Yes, I'm with that group over there," he said as he waved to a small group of men and women.

"Can I treat you to another coffee, Mellie?"

"Yes, that will be nice, thank you, mine's a cappuccino please."

As he was ordering our coffees I couldn't believe that this was the same man whom I thought I knew for two years and was married to for four years, before he left me. Although it felt more or less like being abandoned at the time, with Evie just being two years old. He left me without saying goodbye, not even a note. Neville looked very gaunt. I can't remember him being that slim! He looks in need of a good meal. He doesn't look that healthy either. His hair is very grey and thinning in parts and his teeth need some dental care. He hasn't worn very well. He looks like he's lived a rough life.

He brought the coffees over to where I was sitting.

"Do you mind if we sit somewhere more comfortable and not so public?"

"No, I don't mind Neville, you choose."

We sit down away from his group of friends and somewhere that's a bit quieter and where there's less activity.

"This is so much better. Neville, why do you want to see me?"

"Just like you, Mellie, always wanting direct answers. Just like your mother!"

"Well, yes I do. I haven't got all day. I've got things to do! Please leave my mother out of this. If it wasn't for her, I wouldn't be here meeting you!"

"Yes, I remember, you were always busy. Keep your hair on. There's no offence meant."

"Glad to hear it. I had to be. It was no good us both being laissez faire or laid back. We wouldn't have achieved anything if we had."

"Here you go, still always having to achieve something. Come on Mellie, get a life!"

"My name is Melissa. Stop calling me Mellie!"

"Oh! We are touchy, aren't we? Who's rattled your cage?"

"Don't ask the obvious and expect to get an answer!"

"Can we start again? I'm sorry but I haven't seen you for a long time. I always remember calling you Mellie and you didn't seem to mind back then."

"That's a long time ago, things have changed and so have I!"

"I needed to see you because I would like to meet my daughter, Evie, and I need you to introduce us. There's lots that I need her to know about me. I am her Dad, you know!"

"Yes, I know that, you fool. Now Evie is your daughter! Your daughter! Don't you remember what you used to call her. No, then I will remind you, you called her a BRAT!!! I'm not even sure that she would want to meet you anyway. She doesn't remember you. She never knew you. You made no attempt to get or keep in touch. You never even sent Evie a birthday card! What kind of father does that? You abandoned us. Well, didn't you?"

"Yes, I know and now I'm not proud of what I did. It was bad of me to leave you both as I did, but, at the time, I thought it would be for the best."

"You mean to say it's taken you all this time to realise that? Where have you been?"

"I've travelled the world over a few times. I've seen lots of things. I've done lots of things. Things even I had never imagined doing or even happening to me."

"I'm glad one of us has managed to be happy and free from responsibilities."

"Don't be childish, it doesn't suit you and nor does sarcasm."

"Well, what have you done? I'm dying to hear."

"No, don't die, but I am."

"Why do you want to see Evie?"

"I'm dying. The oncologist has advised two to three months, tops."

"Oh, I didn't realise. Sorry."

"You shouldn't be made to feel sorry. It's not your fault."

"I've done a lot of stupid things with my life. I've been married six times after you to some very beautiful women, plus my first wife before we met, so that makes eight, my lucky number! I hasten to add Evie is my only child, though. It's taken me a long time to recognise and admit that I am gay. For the first time in my life I'm really happy and feel complete. Did you remarry, Melissa?"

"No, I haven't found anyone. After you, I find it very hard to trust men. I've tried over the years but I just can't trust. Any way I've got Evie and she's my world. I don't feel the need for anyone else."

"Will you please have a word with Evie, and if she wants to see me you've got my contact number."

"I promise to tell Evie but I will leave her to decide for herself."

"Fair enough, I can't ask for any more than that. Can I!"

"I want you to promise me that you will not get in touch with Mother again. I don't want to meet up with you ever again. Do you understand what I'm saying?"

"Yes, I promise. Even if Evie doesn't get in touch. I'll respect whatever she decides."

"Good. I hope you keep your word. Now if you don't mind I need to get on with my own life. Just leave me alone."

I have to get out of the cafe/bar. I can't stay there any longer. I need some fresh air. Oh! Neville stinks. I don't tell Neville that Evie lives with her Nan.

As I'm strutting towards the railway station I decide to go and see Mother and Evie in Speckleton before returning home. I think it's best to get this matter sorted once and for all and just knock it on the head. I just hope they're both in.

"Hum that smells nice, and is there room for one more?"

"Hello dear, what a nice surprise," my mother whispered, "have you talked to Neville?"

So I whispered, "Yes, and I've seen him this morning."

"Hey! Why are you two whispering? Perhaps you're talking about me, are YOU?"

"Hi sweetheart, how are you? Come here." We embrace each other and then Mother joins in. A family group hug. My family. That's nice.

"I'm fine, Mum. Nan, can I have some more lunch please? That was delicious."

"Just help yourself dear, but leave a bit for your Mum."

"No, don't be silly, Mother, I'm not that bothered. Really."

"Mum, you look nice but it's not like you to come here dressed casually. In fact the casual look suits you."

"Thank you sweetheart, it's nice to get a compliment from my little girl."

"Don't know if you've noticed but I'm far from being little!"

"You know what I mean, sweetheart."

Evie helps herself to more food and returns to the dining room. Mother has made a pudding and so I have a slice of that with loads of home-made custard, it's not instant, it's real custard, hum.

Mother, seeing the amount of food in my bowl, asks "You must be really hungry dear, did you have any breakfast?"

"No, I didn't feel like having anything earlier. I wasn't looking forward to meeting Neville."

"Well that's understandable, enjoy your pudding then."

"Oh I certainly will. I think you've surpassed yourself. It looks and smells delicious but the proof will be in the eating. Won't it?"

"It should be alright. I've made it many times before."

"Just joking Mother, of course it will, except I've never tried this! It looks wonderful."

"Oh, thank you dear, it's nice to be appreciated."

Mother and I joined Evie in the dining room, she was just having her last mouthful of food.

"That was lovely, Nan." Evie looked like she was about to make an exit.

"What are you doing this afternoon, sweetheart?"

"I'm meeting Sharnie later for a coffee. Why?"

"Evie, I need to have a moment with you, perhaps after I've eaten my pudding."

"I'm just going to have a shower, we can talk while I'm getting ready."

"Lovely, I just want a quick word with your Nan too."

"Ok! Whatever."

"Hum, Mother this is delicious."

"Yes I have to admit it, it is rather good."

Mother and I finish eating our pudding. Our spoons scraping the bowls empty making a clanking noise as we do.

"How did you get on with Neville, dear?"

"Oh, quite a shock. Actually."

"Oh, what do you mean? Enlighten me, won't you?"

"I can't honestly remember Neville being slim and gaunt. He smelt as well. Ugh!"

"Oh dear, what did he want exactly?"

"He wants to meet Evie."

"Oh dear. Evie won't want that!"

"Well, that will be for her to decide. I'll have to tell her; I promised Neville I would. It's only fair."

"Fair! To him or Evie?"

I shrugged my shoulders because I didn't know what to say. I'm on life's emotional roller coaster and I want to get off, but I have to continue.

"I'd better go and speak to Evie, Mother, while she's still here."

"If you need me you'll know where to find me."

"Yes, but it's something I need to do myself. Wish me luck."

"Good luck."

I knocked on Evie's bedroom door.

"Come in Mum, but you don't need to knock!"

I sat on Evie's bed; she was just finishing getting ready.

"What's on your mind, Mum? You look like you've got the world's problems all on your shoulders. What's up?"

It was no good beating about the bush with Evie, she's very much like me and Mother. She needs to be told as it is. A welcome reality check. I didn't think so.

"Ok, sweetheart, your biological father wants to see you. I've got his mobile contact number written on this slip of paper, I'll just leave it on your dressing table. It's up to you."

"I hope you're joking!"

"Evie, this is something which I wouldn't joke about. You know that, don't you?"

"Why? Why has he left it up until now? I don't even remember what he looks like. He's never sent me a birthday card, nor any presents at Christmas, as far back as I can remember, Mum. Why? Why now?"

"I think you'd better ask your Dad that question. He needs to tell you for himself."

"This is something that I need to think over. I'm not going to get in touch with him in a hurry. I need some time. I need to think. You know, I just was thinking the other day, that my life's just beginning to settle and that everything in it is just starting to come together. I never, in a million years, ever gave it a moment's notice, that this man who claims to be my biological father, is now going to ruin every hope of happiness that I ever expected to achieve."

"Look, I think it's best that you find out for yourself with very little input from me. You're mature enough now to decide for yourself."

My heart was going out to my lovely only daughter who I could see was struggling with her conscience about what would be the right thing to do, but I couldn't help thinking that she's old enough now to be able to decide for herself.

"Well, if you need to talk, Evie, you know you can ring me any time, sweetheart. Don't you? You know that I'm a good listener."

"Quite honestly, Mum, I don't want to think about Dad anymore. I'm just going to get on with my life and I'm going now to meet Sharnie as arranged for a chat and a coffee."

"Evie, I just want you to know that whatever you decide it will be alright with me."

"Yes, I know, Mum, and I'm just so grateful that he didn't just turn up here at Nan's."

"Yes, so am I."

"Mum there's something that I need to tell you. Are you ready?"

"Ready, ready for what?"

"Mum, I'm getting married. I'm not going to wait after all!"

"Married! Married! When, sweetheart?"

"Oh, in a few weeks. Don't worry, Charles is organising the wedding, the reception and our honeymoon!"

We both walked through to the kitchen. Mother had tidied up and was now sitting reading a magazine. Evie kissed us both goodbye on her way out.

"How did she take the news, dear?"

"I'll think she'll be alright. She just needs some time to think things over. It has been a bit of a shock for us all really, hasn't it?"

"Yes it has but never mind. We'll deal with it as we usually do as a family."

"Yes, we will. If you don't mind, Mother, I'm going to make my way home; it's been quite a day and I didn't get very much sleep last night. I'm feeling rather tired."

"No, that's alright with me, dear. Take care and I'll be in touch sometime next week."

"Yes, alright Mother. You take care too. Cheerio for now."

"Cheerio, dear."

Mother and I kiss each other on the cheek.

"I gather Evie has told you about her wedding."

"Yes, she did. I only hope that she knows what she's doing."

"She'll be alright. Try not to worry about her."

Evie's getting married. I can't believe it.

I'm now making my way to the railway station to catch the train to Peaty Hallow.

A few weeks later Mother and Evie had gone to a craft centre and bought several packets of crepe paper, with an assortment of pretty pastel colours, and reels of florist's wire. Charles and Evie decided to have a Hawaiian themed wedding to be held at the Jacks' family Estate. So the crepe paper was for me to make paper flowers for me, Mother, Evie, Charles and Frederick. So every opportunity I have, like breaks at work and evenings, I'm making paper flower arm and ankle bands, hair and neck garlands. I've also gained a new skill, faster hands when I concentrate. I've certainly progressed things. Evie and Mother had doubts that I might not get things done in time. It must be the jam that Frederick keeps giving me. I feel so well.

Evie and Mother will be sewing the crepe flowers that I have made onto their items of clothing which they will be wearing at the wedding. Mother will be wearing a short suit and T shirt. I don't know what Evie and Charles will be wearing. I'll have to wait and see. I'll be sewing flowers onto my own clothes and, at the moment, haven't quite made up my mind. I may buy something completely new. Decisions, decisions. Frederick has his own flowers so he will be sorting his own outfit.

Evie decided in the end not to get in touch with her biological father. She thought she would let sleeping dogs lie. After all, he did leave us some eighteen years ago and never ever made any contact with either of us. Now her wedding is taking precedence.

Evie and Charles have instructed his Mum and Dad to invite family and close friends only. Charles wants to keep the guest list to about one hundred guests. He has insisted that he is shown the list but Nigel and Linda found it so difficult to respect this wish. He and Evie will be sending out their own invitations.

The Night Before the Wedding

Mother and Evie will be arriving in a while so I'm organised. I've got to be because there can be no room for errors. I've got a one pot meal bubbling away in my slow cooker so we can eat whenever we want. I just hope that Mother and Evie don't forget anything. Mother should be alright because she has all day to get ready, but I do wonder about Evie. She tends to daydream. Although Mother, providing she has the opportunity, should be able to keep Evie grounded.

Mother and Evie arrive and there's not much luggage.

"Hello, Mother."

"Hello, dear."

"Hi, Evie."

"Hello, Mum."

"You're both travelling light!"

"Yes, Nan's going home tomorrow after my wedding reception. She's got a date."

"A date! Anyone I know?"

"No, just a friend. Someone I've known for a very long time."

"That's wonderful, Mother."

"Well, when Evie moves out I'm going to be a bit lonely. I've not been on my own for a very very long time, so I'm widening my circle of friends."

"We've already dropped off my suitcase ready for going on our honeymoon tomorrow. We couldn't see the point of bringing it here."

"Good, let's get settled in. I hope you're both hungry. Dinner's ready, or ready when you are."

"Smashing, Mum."

"Lovely, dear."

"We're going to have a good night tonight, just the three of us."

"Yes, we will Mum, because I'm not going out tonight."

"Well, I'm glad to hear it."

"I'm looking forward to it, dear."

"Well, we can afford to relax and chill out because as far as I'm aware, we're all ready."

"Yes dear, we are."

"Lovely. Let's get the evening started."

"Let's."

"Mum, can you show me what you are going to wear tomorrow?"

"Oh, can't you wait until tomorrow?"

"No, I'm just curious."

"Whatever your Mum wears she will always look nice."

"Yes, I know."

"Alright, I'm wearing a T shirt and a short suit which I've sown paper flowers on, some really pretty new sandals and I've made a paper flower hair band. I'm accessorising with arm bands and an ankle band. I'm wearing a paper flower garland around my neck."

"Oh, I thought you'd be wearing a bikini and a sarong!"

"No! Not at my age, sweetheart."

"Evie, did you find something?"

"Yes I have but I'm keeping mine under wraps until tomorrow morning. I'll surprise you."

"Mother, have you seen what Evie is going to wear?"

"No, I'm going to have to wait until tomorrow, just like you."

"Right you two, are you hungry?"

"Yes, let's eat, dear."

"Help yourself, everything is ready. I'll open the wine. Let's celebrate."

"Yes let's, Mum."

Wedding Day

Evie and Charles did agree not to see each other before their wedding, they didn't want to tempt fate. Let's hope the day runs smoothly. I'm giving my only daughter away. The two little bridesmaids, Lily aged three, Ella aged five, Belinda's children, will already be at the Jacks'. Frederick will be arriving about half an hour before the wedding car comes for me and Evie. He's escorting Mother and taking her to the estate in his limousine. Frederick's staff have already arrived, a hairdresser named Ann, to fix our hair and June, the beautician, who we have met before, to fix our makeup, nails and feet. Mother's going first, followed by me and Evie will be last. Mother and I thought it would be a good idea if Evie had a lie in considering how late we all were going to bed. We've all got a delicious flute of Frederick's sparkling champagne and he has also sent us a picnic hamper so we can have a nibble. I've loaded my music centre with our favourite CDs so we've already got a party atmosphere while we're getting ready.

It seems strange dressing to go to an Hawaiian Wedding but in a way it's better, it's less formal. Thinking more about it, it should be more fun. The ceremony and the reception will be traditional. Nigel and Linda Jack have arranged for a registrar to direct the marriage proceedings.

There's a knock at the door.

"Mother, can you answer the door, please?"

"Yes, I'm on my way."

Mother answers the door, it's the three bouquets being delivered from the local florists.

"Gosh, these are beautiful. Melissa, you've ordered well, dear. Evie's going to love these. The colours are so vibrant and they smell wonderful."

"I'll have a look later. As you can see I'm not able to at the moment. Not that I'm complaining. Mother, is Evie up yet?"

"I'm just making a pot of tea if anyone's interested. I'm going to take a cup to Evie."

Mother goes into Evie's room and comes right back out still with the cup of tea in her hand. Mother's expression says it all.

"Evie's not in her room but I can guess where she is."

"Mother, can you give her a ring please, she'll need to get ready. How long will it be, Ann, before you've finished with me?"

She replies, "Oh, about ten minutes."

Mother phones Evie and demands that she comes back within the next ten minutes. Evie promises to return, she walked down to the estate to have a look at the decorations in the two rooms where her wedding and reception will be held. She told Mother that Charles is going to bring her back. My little monkey, she never did enjoy surprises.

By the time I'm ready, Evie's being worked on, and Mother is attempting to finish our champagne.

Frederick arrives wearing his top hat, a short suit, T shirt and a tailed jacket.

"Oh, Mother, look what Frederick is wearing."

"I'm going to let him in."

"Hello Frederick, how are you dear?"

"I'm fine, Nancy, thank you. You're looking very Hawaiian."

"Thank you, dear. It's good to see that you have a sense of humour, dear."

"You don't think it's a tad too formal, do you?"

"No, you look quite the gentleman."

"Thank you, Nancy."

I couldn't stop laughing, Frederick looked so funny. A short man in a very tall hat.

"I'm so sorry, but I never imagined that you'd be wearing top hat and tails. You look so funny. Oh, I'm glad you're here though. Come here."

I kissed Frederick on the lips. This was our first kiss in public. I could almost feel Mother's eyes searing into us but, you know what, I didn't care. I can't be sure but I think Frederick felt the same.

"You look very Hawaiian too, my dear."

"Well thank you, kind sir."

When the wedding car arrives Evie makes her entrance. Mother and I are speechless. The tears start to well up in my eyes, Evie looks so beautiful.

Frederick says, "Evie, you look absolutely stunning."

"Thank you, Frederick."

"You look smart."

"Thank you, Evie."

I notice that Mother is wiping her eyes very carefully, so as not to disturb her makeup, and agrees "Yes, she does."

Frederick cuddles me and I feel better.

"Evie, sweetheart, you look so serene."

Mother adds, "Our little princess."

Frederick and I both agree.

"Well, Nancy, are you ready to go?"

"Yes, I'm ready."

Frederick escorts Mother to his limousine.

I pass Evie her bouquet which completes her outfit. I pick up the two bridesmaids' bouquets and we make our way to the wedding car. The chauffeur opens one of the doors as we approach. While Evie is getting in I walk around the back of the wedding car and get in. The chauffeur closes both the doors and within a few minutes we're on our way. I look out of the back window and Frederick's limousine is travelling behind us. I smile at Evie and she smiles back. The flowers in the back window of the wedding car match Evie's bouquet. Good.

"I'm so very proud of you, Evie."

"Oh, Mum, you'll have me crying in a minute."

I take hold of Evie's hand and we hold hands all the way to the Estate.

"I like Frederick's outfit, Mum. He's so eccentric."

On arrival at the estate we are met and greeted by Linda and Nigel Jack and two photographers, one with a camcorder and one with a camera. The two bridesmaids are given their bouquets and Linda helps me with Evie's outfit. Once we have conquered the steps up to the hallway, we are greeted by Charles and the registrar, who is a lady.

"Oh, Evie, darling, you are beautiful and I am extremely lucky that you have agreed to be my wife." Charles kisses Evie.

"You two need to come with me. You both need to complete some of the paperwork before the ceremony can take place. This is the official side to your wedding so if you could step this way please. We can start getting things processed," instructed the registrar.

Evie gave me her bouquet. Linda and I folded Evie's train and we wait patiently for Evie and Charles to return to us.

Nigel and Frederick escort Mother into the room where the ceremony is taking place.

"I'm afraid she's had a little too much champagne," I say.

I can hear Hawaiian music being played and it sounds wonderful.

When Evie, Charles and the registrar return, the registrar escorts Charles into the room. Linda and I straighten out Evie's train.

"Are you alright, sweetheart?"

"Yes, Mum, I'm fine. I think wedding nerves are kicking in."

"Take a couple of deep breaths," Linda advises.

I pick up Evie's bouquet and hand it to her.

"That's a really beautiful bouquet, Evie," compliments Linda.

"Yes, it is. Mum must have the credit for the bouquets. She chose the flowers and the design on my behalf. I wouldn't know where to start."

"Good luck, Evie, I'm going to join Nigel but if you don't mind I'm going to sprinkle some rose petals as I go."

"No, Linda, I don't mind at all. Thank you."

"That's a very nice gesture Evie. Isn't it?"

"Yes, it's a nice surprise, Mum. Now are you ready, Mum?"

"Yes, Evie, let's get things moving."

We hold onto each other and gently we move forward, with the two bridesmaids following behind us, until we are just inside the door. We all stop and we wait for the Hawaiian Steel Guitar to play 'The Wedding March.' Everyone's eyes are looking straight at us. Evie and I are smiling as we walk up the middle of the room in time to the music.

The room looks absolutely marvellous. The Jacks have excelled themselves and done us proud. The flowers have been beautifully displayed and they smell absolutely wonderful. As we pass by the wedding guests, one by one, on both sides of our path, they approve Evie's outfit as we walk by. Some nod their heads, others smile, some mime, "You look lovely."

Evie and I smile, nod and mime, "Thank you" as we go by.

Charles and Harvey have turned around and they both avidly watch us as we get closer and closer. Harvey seems to approve Evie's outfit. He whispers to Charles.

Charles agrees and I can see the love that he feels for my daughter expressed in his face. When we join them the registrar asks me, "Are you giving Evie away?"

I simply reply, "Yes, I am."

The registrar takes Evie's hand away from mine, and places it on Charles' hand. I join Mother and Frederick and my eyes begin to well up with tears. Frederick takes my hand and gently squeezes it. He asks me if I'm alright. I nod my head and smile.

The ceremony begins, everything goes as it should until the registrar asks, "If anyone here present knows of any reason why Charles and Evie cannot be joined together as man and wife, speak now or forever hold your peace."

Then Iris shouts out, "Sorry but I'm just about to have our baby. My waters have just broken. I'm sorry for the mess. Ben, can you ring for an ambulance please?"

Linda took hold of one of Iris's arms and Ben took the other so that they could both support her. They escorted her out of the room.

Once Linda returned to her seat the wedding ceremony continued. Nigel gently touched Linda's shoulder and whispered, "Is Iris going to be alright?"

Linda nods her head and whispers, "Yes, I think so."

The ceremony continues and after the registrar pronounces Charles and Evie, man and wife, Charles kisses his wife for the first time. It's now time for Charles, Evie, me, Linda and Nigel to go and sign the register, followed by the two photographers. Once this is done all the formalities are now complete and my daughter is now officially Mrs Evie Jack.

When the ceremony is over all the guests are directed to the main hall where the reception is being held. As Mother, Frederick and I make our way through to the reception we notice Iris and Ben making their way towards a waiting ambulance.

Once we are in the main hall, wow! The Jacks have certainly surpassed themselves, yet again. They certainly know how to throw a party. They've captured the Hawaiian scene beautifully and someone has been very busy. Along the back of the top table there's a painted beach scene backdrop so it looks like we're having the wedding breakfast on the beach. Down the length of one of the other walls there are real palm trees planted in patio containers. It looks like the guests will be seated on picnic tables which are randomly spaced so there are no straight lines. On the table tops there are small colourful floral decorations and pretty foil confetti sprinkles which sparkle in the light.

I kiss Frederick and say, "I'll see you both later," leaving Mother and Frederick to find where they are seated.

I join Evie, Charles, Nigel and Linda who have already formed a line ready to greet the wedding guests into the reception Hawaiian style by saying "Aloha." Linda introduces me to the guests that she knows and I introduce Linda to my family and some of Evie's friends. When all the guests and family are in the room we all make our way over to the top table.

"Mum, have you seen the wedding cake?"

"Yes, I went to the bakers to inspect it last week and gave them my approval, it wasn't assembled, I viewed three cakes. Why?"

"It's wonderful, Mum. I love your design and I adore the bride and groom. Thank you, Mum."

"I'm glad you like it."

I could see the cake from where I am sitting. It is displayed on the end of the top table on the Jacks' side away from all the chaos. It is good to see it assembled into three tiers. The cake is a rich fruit cake which is flavoured through with brandy. It's covered with almond paste with a top layer of royal icing. The bride and groom standing on top of the cake are clothed Hawaiian style. The groom is wearing a white jacket, black shorts, a brightly coloured Hawaiian T shirt and flip-flops. The bride is wearing a pink bikini, white robe and flip-flops. Both the bride and groom are wearing hair garlands. The two lower tiers are covered with brightly coloured flowers and sea shells. All the decorations on the cake are edible.

Food and drinks are served. There is a choice of starters, melon balls with a champagne sorbet or prawn cocktail. The main course choice is either roast beef or roast turkey with all the trimmings. The choice of desserts is Hawaiian fruit salad with cream or ice cream, or a triple chocolate layered gateau. There is red or white wine and a choice of non-alcoholic drinks.

Then came the time for the speeches. I'd already made it known that I wasn't going to make any speech because I didn't think it was necessary. Harvey started off by welcoming family and friends to the reception of

117

his brother, Charles and his new sister-in-law, Evie. He welcomed her into the Jack family. He avoids embarrassing Charles with stories from Charles' past, like ex-girlfriends. He wishes Charles and Evie all the happiness that they both deserve. He reads a few e-mails from those guests who couldn't come to the wedding. He hopes Charles and Evie would have a great Hawaiian honeymoon. He finishes by hoping that everyone will have a wonderful time and thanks everyone for all the wedding presents.

Most of us put our hands together and clap, giving approval to Harvey's heartfelt and somewhat short speech.

Charles and Evie cut into their wedding cake and three caterers came and took the cake, presumably to the kitchen. All the guests were offered a slice of cake. Hum, it is scrummy.

There is someone arguing in the hallway, their voices get louder and louder. Then the door bursts open and in barges Neville, mouthing his head off, and is immediately pursued by two security guards. Neville is wearing a suit, he looks very smart, but he looks quite out of place.

"Get your hands off me, I want to see my daughter!"

"Sir, you haven't got an invitation so you are not welcome to join this party."

"You don't seem to understand. I Want To See My Daughter!"

"Sir, you need to come with us."

"Evie, Evie, I want to see you," he shouted.

One of the security guards managed to handcuff Neville and they started to lead him out of the room.

Evie has obviously heard her father so she follows them. Charles, wondering what is happening, instinctively follows Evie.

I was really mortified because he had promised to honour Evie's decision and I couldn't help thinking how he knew or found out about Evie's wedding. I certainly didn't mention this to him when I met him in Tinville. So how the hell did he find out? Nigel and Linda were also confused and were wondering what was going on. I felt awful but didn't quite know what to say. So I made a quick exit from the top table and I walked over to where Mother and Frederick were sitting. Mother was having a conversation with Frederick; she might have been explaining to him what had just happened. I needed some answers and I thought that Mother could enlighten me, so I butted in.

"Mother, how did Neville find out about Evie's wedding?"

Mother very reluctantly replies, "I told him. Why?"

"Mother, you shouldn't have told him. Evie didn't want to see her father and you should have respected that. You shouldn't have interfered. What were you thinking?"

"Well, I thought that Neville ought to know. It was up to him whether he came or not! Wasn't it?"

"Quite honestly, Mother, you should have respected Evie's decision."

Mother replied quite indignantly, "So!"

I was absolutely furious with Mother; my temper was raging. Our eyes locked for a few minutes. Then I make a quick exit, I need to get some fresh air. I feel like I'm suffocating in my mother's presence. I also need a bit of time by myself to try and cool down.

There are a few guests who have come outside to have a cigarette. There is a special designated area for smokers.

Frederick joined me after making sure that Mother was alright.

"How are you, sweetheart?"

"I'm getting there. I never thought for one moment that Mother would do anything like this."

"She thought she was doing the right thing."

"You know I've never turned Evie against her father, in fact, the opposite."

"Come here Melissa, let me comfort you."

Frederick wrapped his arms around me and the world seemed to be a safer place. He gently wiped my tears with his handkerchief and sweetly kissed my face. I started to kiss Frederick and some of my worries just seemed to melt away.

"You know' Frederick' I just feel like going home."

"Then, why don't you?"

"Because I really want to spend more time with Evie. Every moment that I spend with my daughter is so precious."

"Come on, Melissa, let's go and join the others. Let's celebrate. Don't let your mother or Neville spoil this day. What do you say?"

"I'm so glad that I found you, Frederick. I'm so grateful. It will be a while before I can fully forgive Mother for what she's done. You're so right, we should celebrate."

"Then come on, Melissa, what's stopping you?"

"Frederick, there's just something I want to say to you."

Frederick's eyes look straight into mine. I encase his face with both my hands and say, "Frederick, I love you."

"I know you do, Melissa, and I love you too. I only wish that I could have told you first."

We kiss each other and for me it's wonderful.

"Right, let's go and join the others."

Frederick puts his arm around me and I put my arm around him. I think finally we are a couple.

On the way back to the wedding reception Frederick and I both notice a group of young people messing about with mobile phones, they must be quite drunk because they're very boisterous and creating some ridiculous poses.

"There must be a camera or two in those phones, they're obviously taking 'selfies'," Frederick says.

When we join the reception I notice that Evie has removed her wedding gown and is now wearing a very frilly pink and lilac bikini. She's also wearing a white sarong around her waist. Charles has taken off his jacket and the pair of them look quite relaxed.

The Hawaiian Steel Guitar music resumes again and Charles leads Evie onto the dance floor and they dance 'The Hula'. The pair of them must have had dancing lessons. They do look good. They also have their first waltz too as husband and wife. Evie looks so happy and relaxed and so does Charles. After their favourite music ends, the music picks up a beat and becomes much livelier, some of the other guests now join them on the dance floor. Frederick asks me to dance and I accept.

Evie and Charles leave their reception to get ready to go on their honeymoon. A taxi has been booked to take them to the airport.

Evie returns to the reception and she asks to see me alone. So we find somewhere quiet away from the celebration.

"Mum, I just want you to know that I don't bear any grudges against Nan. I really think she had my interests at heart. I can see why she decided to contact my dad, father, oh whatever you'd like to call him. I've told him to his face that I don't want anything more to do with him. After all the shouting he's agreed to let me go and I want to show you this. He's given me his mother's gold locket and there are photographs of his mother and father inside. Here, look."

"Yes, I remember that his mother wore this locket when she was alive. You won't remember them, sweetheart, you were very young. I didn't keep in touch with them after your father left us. They couldn't see their son as I did. It was very nice of him I suppose to give you that locket."

"Yes, that's what I think. Mum, before you go I just want to say thank you for everything. Charles and I really appreciate all that you've done for us today. Thank you."

"That's alright, sweetheart, it was a pleasure. Come here."

We cuddle and kiss each other.

"Now, young lady, you've got a honeymoon to go too. Come, let's go and join the others while you and Charles wait for your taxi."

We have only just returned to the reception when one of the security guards announces the arrival of the taxi.

We all follow Evie and Charles. Nigel helps the driver put their luggage in the boot. While some of the guests shower them with rice and rose petals. Evie and Charles get into the taxi and I just have time to say, "I hope you both have a nice time and see you when you come back. Bye."

Linda is standing alongside me and she says, "Ditto."

The taxi disappears down the driveway. We both wave until we can't see it anymore.

When I turn around Frederick and Mother are not far from where I'm standing.

I smile at Frederick and I join them.

"What time are you going home, Mother?"

"My taxi is booked to arrive at yours in about an hour's time."

"Frederick, what time is your limousine arriving?"

123

"I haven't told James a specific time. He will now be somewhere in the village. All I need to do is give him a ring. He could be here in a matter of minutes."

"Oh good, can you do that then, please?"

"Mother, we just need to say our goodbyes to the Jack family."

"I'm not going back into the reception. I don't want to go up those steps any more. They're playing havoc with my knees. Could you bring Evie's bouquet for me; she said that I could have it?"

"Yes, of course I can. I won't be long."

I return to the reception and I pick up Evie's bouquet from where Mother and Frederick were sitting. I see Linda and Nigel, they're both talking to Belinda, Harvey and their two grandchildren.

I go over to them and say, "Hi, I've just come over to say a big thank you to you both for all you've done today. I just want you to know it's greatly appreciated."

"That's ok, Melissa, it's our pleasure. Oh, by the way Iris has just given birth to our third grandchild."

"Oh I'm so pleased."

"Yes, Ben's just phoned. He says that Iris is fine and it's a boy!"

"Good, I'm so pleased."

"Yes, so are we. It's been quite an eventful day, hasn't it?"

"Yes, I suppose it has, anyway I'm going to say cheerio for now. Mother's got her taxi booked to collect her from mine in under an hour. Take care. Bye."

"Yes, I think we're all going to the hospital in a minute to see our new family member. We were just working out if we could all fit into one vehicle safely. Anyway, Melissa, cheerio. See you soon, perhaps."

"Yes, bye."

When I get outside Frederick's limousine is waiting for me. Frederick and Mother are already in it.

"Oh, by the way, Iris and Ben have a son."

"That's nice, dear. It didn't take long either. When I gave birth to you I was in labour for twenty-four hours."

"Yes, I know. I was a long time giving birth to Evie, if you remember."

"Yes, I remember."

I look into my Mother's eyes but I still can't forgive her.

We arrive at my cottage. Frederick asks John to wait for him.

Mother collects up all of her things and packs them into her wheelie.

"Mother, do you want any more of my special jam?"

"Oh yes, that would be nice, dear. I have used all that you gave me a while ago. When I was here last I should have asked for some more but I forgot."

"That might be why your knees are playing you up. You know. Here you are, take these."

"Are you sure you can afford to let me have those?"

"Yes, I've got plenty left. Anyway I'll be making some more soon."

"Lovely dear, thank you."

"You're welcome."

"Nancy, your taxi is here," Frederick advised.

"Thank you, Frederick."

Frederick and I escort Mother to her waiting taxi. The driver puts her wheelie in the boot. We both wave her goodbye.

As we're walking down my driveway Frederick asks me if I'm alright.

"I'll be alright, Frederick. I just need to change into some other clothes and then I should start tidying up."

"Melissa, will it be alright for me to stay with you tonight? I will have to go back tomorrow, maybe I can give you a hand with the tidying up."

"If you want to. Yes, why not?"

"I'll just tell James to come back tomorrow morning, shall I?"

"Yes, alright."

I went inside. All I felt liked doing was to get out of my wedding clothes, to have a shower and be comfortable. This is what I did.

Frederick had tidied and restored some order in the kitchen and it looked immaculate. He was looking in the fridge and freezer to see what food he could cook us for dinner. He'd already found some wine and by what was left in the bottle he'd had at least a couple of glasses.

"Would you like to change and have a shower, Frederick?"

"Yes, I might, but as you will notice all I have are the clothes that I'm wearing. I don't even have my toothbrush."

"I've already found you some clothes. Mine. They'd fit you. I have spare toothbrushes and I've left one out for you, and it's new!"

"Yes, I could do with changing my clothes. Do you have anything for my feet?"

"Sorry, no can do."

"Never mind, I'll have a shower and put my socks back on my feet."

"Oh, wait a minute, I'm not thinking straight. I thought you wanted something like slippers. I have plenty of clean socks, perhaps the ones that I wear when I'm gardening will fit."

"I'll get us something to eat when I've had a shower. Thanks, sweetheart."

"You're welcome. I've left you some clean towels in the bathroom. The clothes are on top of my bed."

"Thanks."

While I was talking to Frederick I poured myself a glass of wine. When Frederick was having his shower, I retired to the conservatory and sat drinking my wine, looking out at my garden. Moggie came in and sat on my lap, I started to stroke her and she started to purr, that was magic to my ears, I felt myself starting to unwind.

Lovely. The thoughts of Neville just turning up today, and my Mother's interference, were beginning to melt away.

When Frederick had finished he came through and found me in the conservatory. Moggie took an instant dislike to Frederick. She raised herself on all fours cursing Frederick then she jumped off my lap and ran outside cursing again as she went.

"Sorry, Frederick, she's never done that!"

"Don't let it worry you, all cats that don't know me do that. It doesn't worry me anymore! Now let's get dinner. Can you prepare the vegetables?"

"Yes, I've got something to show you."

A few vegetables were there in front of me. I placed some of them on a chopping board and with a sharp knife I started to chop. I just thought 'I wish I could chop faster' and within a few seconds all the vegetables were chopped and witnessed by Frederick.

"Wow! Looks like my jam is working for you."

"It is that, that's causing this?"

"Yes, I would say so. Yippee. Let's celebrate."

"Should we?"

"Yes, of course, because it means that my jam is compatible with your body and it should work in a positive way."

"Oh, what would happen if it was incompatible then?"

"Well the side effects are different for each individual. Normally if someone doesn't like the appearance of the jam or doesn't like how the jam tastes then obviously it wouldn't be a good idea to even try consuming the jam. Another variable is the jam may not be compatible with the body if it is consumed one day and not another or eaten for, say, one week continuously, then having a break. Another variable is if a person has too much jam, say, for instance, a comfort eating disorder and continues on a regular basis, then a person may start to hallucinate and if that person doesn't stop then their symptoms could spiral into depression and other mental health issues. So you can see it's very much down to each individual. That's why we couldn't say anything to anyone else, except for you, my dear, you're alright."

"Hum, this is very interesting and you certainly now have my attention. Frederick, is this what you and your family have experienced?"

"Yes, but what I've just told you has taken years to find out and to understand. When my Papa and Mama first started to consume the Tinsel tree jam they didn't know. They ate the jam and drank the wine out of necessity. When Mama could see that my Papa was still alive after consuming the syrup she allowed us all to pour it over our porridge and we thrived on it. It must have boosted our immunity because we didn't suffer from the common cold, flu, the pox, or anything nasty like the others with whom we came into contact. Papa and Mama could see that we children were growing and developing as we should, so we all continued consuming the syrup. When I, Florry and Beatrice were in our teens we all started consuming the jam. In the time in which my family lived adults didn't live for very long. Some women died in childbirth, some would catch the fever, or pox, my list is endless but you get the point. If, like us, you were lucky you might be expected to have lived until about the age of forty-five, some did survive until they were fifty-two, but this was very rare and you were thought of, by others, as being extremely lucky. Papa realised when he reached the age of seventy something unusual was happening, but he was alive, felt extremely well and his body was strong. He lived each day as though it might be his last but he continued to work as a builder. Mama and Papa do not mention their ages to anyone as they don't want to draw attention to themselves; as children we were never aware of their age, we celebrated their birthdays but were totally ignorant of how old they were. In fact, back then it was considered to be most impolite and disrespectful to ask the age of another person. Mama and Papa just quietly got on with their lives."

Frederick has certainly got my full attention and I'm still wondering whether to believe his story or not. At this moment I do not discuss my thoughts with Frederick. In fact, I'm totally lost for words.

"Do you have any religious beliefs?"

"Our family had to be careful not to admit to any specific religion. Back then England was divided by all different factions of people with different views regarding religious beliefs and some paid with their lives. My Mama and Papa chose not to speak of or admit to having any religious beliefs, by, maybe, appearing neutral. Quietly our family believe in giving praises to the earth. Papa has often, quietly, mentioned to us that all the different types of religions here on the earth represent all different modes of transport which are all going to the same destination. In other words, whatever anyone's religious beliefs are they will all go to heaven."

"Hum, very interesting. That's why none of you were burnt at the stake then."

"Well, yes, I suppose. I don't know. I was too young to understand at the time. By the way this is something that my Mama and Papa don't talk about."

CHAPTER VI

I'm on my way, travelling by train, to see Frederick. Over the past few weeks our relationship is becoming more intense; we are no longer close friends. We are now almost lovers.

Frederick has invited me to spend the day with him and he's sent me a return train ticket. He's arranged for his chauffeur to pick me up from the station and to take me to The Guest House for luncheon. Sounds very posh.

I'm really looking forward to being with him. He makes me feel really special. He's such a gentle and kind man. I feel that I know him really well or at least I think I do. I feel that he's always giving me one hundred and ten percent of his attention. He really listens to me and we have a really good dialogue between us. He has a very soft and sensual way with words and, oh, his lovely soft voice seems to have a really soothing effect on me. The way he speaks to me is almost poetic. He never ceases to fascinate me because he really is fascinating. The more I'm in his company the more I want to be in his company. Even when he holds my hand he does it in a most gentle and sensitive manner. I love the way that he caresses my hand when we are alone. It feels so natural, spontaneous and private. He moves me, he makes my body tingle. I feel that I can really trust him now and you know what, I do!

"Can I see your ticket please, miss?"

"Oh sorry, I was deep in thought." I then reach into my bag and pull out my purse. I hand the ticket to the conductor. He checks it and he pops it into his ticket machine and it snips the corner. He then hands it back.

"Thank you, miss. Have a pleasant journey."

"Thank you."

I put the ticket back in my purse to keep it safe. It might get lost in my handbag. Anyway my purse is a much safer place. I resume looking out the window but check my watch beforehand. I don't want to overshoot my destination. It looks like I'll be travelling a little while longer.

When I get off the train James, Frederick's chauffeur, is on the platform waiting for me.

"Hello, James."

"Good afternoon, madam. Do you have any luggage?"

"No, I'm not staying. I'm only here for the day."

"If you follow me, madam, I'll take you to The Guest House."

"Thank you, James."

So I follow him out of the station and into the station car park.

"Wow." I just can't contain myself because there before me is an immaculate Rolls Royce; it shines.

James opens the back door and I get in. Inside was just as good, for me this is the epitome of perfection.

"Alright James, let's go and don't spare the horses."

"Alright, madam."

I could see that Frederick was waiting near the front entrance for me as the Roller drew close by; he was holding a beautiful posy. I get out. Frederick's face bursts out into a cute smile.

"Hello Frederick, what a lovely welcome."

"Good morning, my sweet special lady. I've picked this posy especially for you from our garden."

"These are lovely. Oh they smell wonderful. Thank you."

Frederick reaches for my hand and as he draws it close to his face, he softly says,

"Did you have a pleasant journey?"

"Yes I did. Thank you. Thank you for the ticket. I really appreciate it."

"You're very welcome, Melissa," as he caresses my hand, closing his eyes as he does.

When he opens his eyes he notices me gazing at him. I'm really happy here and I just want to capture each moment. He sees me smiling and for the first time he strokes my face and his hand rests under my chin. He's gazing directly into my eyes and for one moment time seems to slow down. I'm thinking he's going to kiss me. It feels like he's studying my face, every fine line exposed.

"Yes, I am wearing make-up. This is my natural look."

These comments seemed to jerk him back into the real world.

"You have a lovely, kind, open face and your features contrast this."

"Thank you. You're very kind, sir."

"No really, just telling you the truth. Melissa, I will never lie to you. I hope you can trust me, dear lady, I'm not like the others you've mentioned."

"I know that you're not and, Frederick, can I just say, without beating about the bush, I do trust you, there I said it." I start to blush and I am rather hoping that my complexion remains a pretty pink because ruddy red doesn't look very good on me.

He didn't say a word but he certainly noticed. He takes my hand and leads me inside The Guest House.

"I want you to come with me, Melissa," he says, as we go over to the lift.

"Where are we going?"

"I think it's time for you to meet my family. Come with me."

I don't know what I'm expecting but I've often wondered what it would be like meeting Frederick's family and now I'm going to find out.

"We need to go up in the lift. Please follow me dear."

It didn't take long for the lift to arrive. Frederick pressed the top button and the lift moves slowly up.

Once the lift stops, the doors open, Frederick leads me down a corridor until we reach the door to Frederick's family suite. Frederick knocks on the door. A lady's voice says "Come in."

"After you, Melissa."

As I enter the room I am aware that Frederick is following very closely behind. I don't know what I'm expecting to see. Once we're inside I feel that the room I'm now in is probably a reception area. The room, its fittings, its furniture, its decor is very modern and minimalistic.

I was expecting to see two extremely old-looking parents but it is quite the contrary.

"Everyone, I want you all to meet my very dear friend, Melissa."

"It's good to meet you, Melissa, Frederick's told me all about you. By the way my name's Martha. I'm Frederick's Mama."

"Martha, it's really nice to meet you too." I offer my hand and Martha squeezes my hand very gently.

She's quite short in stature and is extremely smart in appearance. Immaculate, in fact. She has a very fair and clear complexion and she has very defined facial features.

"Hi Melissa, I'm Beatrice, Frederick's sister or one of them at least."

"Hello, it's nice to meet you too."

"You know Frederick, Melissa looks remarkably like Catherine. The likeness is really quite scary," Martha says.

"Yes, I know she does," replies Frederick.

I start to feel that I'm under a microscope and am beginning to feel very self-conscious.

Frederick offers me a glass of home-made lemonade. It looks very refreshing so I take it. There's a nice slice of lemon balancing over the rim. My throat is becoming a bit dry so I take a sip. Hum, it's delicious.

"Lovely home-made lemonade. Thank you."

"It's debateable whether the lemonade is really home-made or not, because all I did was to chuck a few lemons into a machine and lemonade comes down the spout, but I did slice a couple of lemons," Beatrice advises.

"Well, it's very refreshing. Thank you."

"Melissa, I would like you to meet my Papa."

"Very good to see you, I'm Rowan by the way."

"Hello, Rowan, I'm very pleased to meet you."

Rowan is a bit taller than me and he is a fine gentleman. His face is clean shaven and looks very smooth. I don't notice any designer stubble present on his face. I do notice that he has very avid eye contact which does send shivers up and down my spine. He too is dressed immaculately and he's wearing a three piece grey suit.

"Melissa, have you seen a likeness of Catherine?" asks Beatrice.

"No, I haven't, but Frederick has already mentioned that I do look very similar to her."

Beatrice shows me a small enamelled portrait of Catherine and it looks like I'm looking at my own reflection. If I believed in reincarnation I would have said that I was indeed Catherine.

"Even I'm astounded. I don't know what to say."

As I'm speaking I feel quite faint; the energy seems to drain right out of me. I can hear Frederick saying. "Melissa, are you alright, sweetheart?"

I must have fainted because when I open my eyes Frederick is kneeling beside me and is holding a small pot of smelling salts.

"She looks very pale," I hear Martha saying.

"Yes, it's like she's seen a ghost!" observes Beatrice.

"That's why I've never shown Melissa Catherine's likeness," says Frederick.

Luckily I'd finished with the lemonade before seeing Catherine's portrait.

I was assisted to a chair with Frederick holding one side and Beatrice holding on to the other.

"Are you alright, Melissa?" Frederick asks.

"Yes, it was just a shock. I'm so sorry. I've spoilt this occasion."

"Here, Melissa, have this," Rowan says as he hands me a small glass of whisky.

"Thank you."

I drink it and I'm beginning to feel a tad better.

"Don't feel too bad, Melissa. It wasn't your fault. There will, hopefully, be other occasions when we will see you again," says Martha.

"I'm so sorry, Melissa, it was a little insensitive of me. Please forgive me."

"I must admit it was a shock at first but I'm alright now."

"So you have no harsh feelings towards me then, Melissa."

"No, I don't think so."

"So can we be friends?"

"Of course we can."

"Frederick, when Melissa is feeling a little better perhaps you should take her out in the garden for some fresh air."

"Yes Papa, I think that will be a good idea. By the way, where's Florence?"

"Oh, she's gone down to the kitchen. There's a bit of a crisis, the dishwasher isn't working again. Sidney is threatening to walk out if it's not fixed soon," Martha advises.

"Yes, that's something that we all need to discuss. We need to get another," insists Frederick.

"We'll wait to see what Florry says when she comes back," says Rowan.

"I'll go down to the kitchen on the way out and have a word with Florry myself."

"Well it's not that vital is it? Why can't Sidney wash the pots in the sink, for heaven's sake?" asks Martha.

"Yes, he's going to have to until we can sort this matter out," advises Rowan.

"Are you feeling better now, Melissa?" asks Frederick.

"Yes I am."

"Then let's go, sweetheart."

Frederick offers his arm and I hold on to him.

"It's been very nice to have met you," I say.

"If you're ready, Melissa," Frederick prompts.

"Yes, I'm good to go."

When we get downstairs Frederick finds somewhere for me to sit in reception. He goes to the kitchen to find out what's going on and to see how Florence is coping.

The reception is busy as usual and I sit watching people coming in and some going out and there are a few guests still checking out. They're very relaxed here because guests don't need to check out until 12 noon. I notice a couple of cleaners reporting to reception and one of the receptionists gives a piece of paper to one of them. They look at the list and then they make their way over to the lift.

Frederick returns to me.

"Did you get things sorted out, Frederick?"

"Yes, Florry has managed to get things sorted. I don't need to be here now."

He offers his arm and I take it and we stroll outside. He leads me along the garden path away from The Guest House.

We don't say a word but I am admiring the garden and my posy. We then reach a fork in the path. Usually we go right which eventually leads back to The Guest House but today, for the first time, we take the other path.

"Oh! We're going a different way."

Frederick is now firmly holding my hand.

"I have something to show you, sweet lady."

After a few minutes of walking we come out of the trees and there's a delightful cottage. It is enchanting. Just out of some glossy magazine.

"Wow. This is a perfect setting."

"Dear lady, this is where I live. This is my home."

"It's so peaceful. It's quieter here than at my own home. It's wonderful."

Frederick opens the front door and he invites me in. He takes the flowers from my arm and I follow him into the kitchen. He puts the posy in a vase of water.

"Gosh! What a super kitchen. I've always wished for a kitchen just like this. I wasn't aware that you lived here. I was under the impression that you lived at The Guest House."

"Oh no, I need my own space, away from it all. I thrive on peace and tranquillity," Frederick says while he washes his hands. He then non verbally gestures to me to follow him.

I see that at the other end of the kitchen there's a rather large conservatory. On my way I notice that the kitchen is extremely modern in design and Frederick hasn't spared any expense in installing all mod cons to suit his culinary skills. I'm really impressed.

Once in the conservatory Frederick is at the table and has already opened a bottle of wine and is pouring it into the glasses.

"This is my own special reserve and I want to share it with you, Melissa. Come and sit here. I've just got to fetch the food from the fridge. I've prepared a cold buffet, nothing too heavy. I'll be a moment."

Once seated, I sip some wine, and it's delicious. I reach across the table to see what kind of wine it is. It must be home-made because the label is handwritten 'family's own special brew'."

Frederick brings in a tray offering a variety of cold cuts, sliced pork pie and sliced scotch eggs. He also brings in a small bowl of baked potatoes with bubbly cheese on top which, by the way, smells wonderful. He goes back into the kitchen and returns with a bowl of home-grown salad.

"Frederick, it must be really satisfying to be completely self-sufficient, knowing exactly where your meat, etcetera, comes from."

"Well, of course it is but it does take time to get things just right. Living off the land has its rewards but it also, at times, comes at a price, but I'm not going to bore you now with all that. Let's eat and enjoy ourselves. Shall we?"

"This wine is delicious. Do you make it on the estate?"

"No, my family have been making this for years. This wine is especially for the family and I'd hoped you would like it. Now tell me what you've been getting up to since I saw you last."

We engage in polite exchanges of conversation while enjoying the delicious food and wine. As time goes by, and the more time we spend in each other's company, our conversation becomes more familiar and less orchestrated. We are both now very relaxed in each other's company.

Our inhibitions seem to be melting away. Frederick has now loosened his tie. With lunch now complete we tidy away the remaining food, cutlery and crockery.

"That was a very splendid lunch, Frederick, thank you very much. Everything was delicious."

"I'm glad you liked it. I just feel that I want to spend some quality time with you, sweet Melissa, and to be alone for a change away from everyone else."

"Yes, I agree, it's been really lovely just us and nobody else."

"Would you like some dessert now?"

"No, I'm really replete. Perhaps we could have some later. I'd love a coffee just to finish off though."

"Yes, I fancy a coffee. I'll just start the machine. When that green light comes on you can choose which type you want."

"Goodness gracious, I have a choice. Oh yes, I'll have a latte. I'm just going to relax in the conservatory."

I sit down at the piano and start to play. While I'm playing I can't help but admire the view of the lake. I'm now realising that Frederick's home is designed to take this view into consideration. I feel so peaceful and the lake looks so tranquil.

Frederick comes into the conservatory with two hot glasses of coffee. Mine looks really good. He puts the coffee down on a small table close by and he joins me on the piano seat. He recognises the tune I'm playing and he sings along. He has a very remarkable voice. When we finish I go over and pick up my glass of coffee.

"Oh thank you, Frederick, this looks lovely."

I sit down on the comfy settee and he follows me over and says,

"This is nice."

"Yes, it is."

While I am drinking my coffee, Frederick gets off the settee and goes over to his music centre and he chooses a romantic CD.

"Would you like to dance, Melissa?"

"Oh, I'd love to, dear Frederick."

"I do love to dance, you know, and it's so nice that you enjoy dancing too. This is rather nice."

"Yes, it's the same with me."

As we spoke we were looking into each other's eyes and with no distractions or interruptions we were enjoying ourselves, happy in each other's company. Frederick is stroking my arm, something which he's never done before.

"This is nice," I whisper.

"Do you want to stop?"

"No! Let's go with the moment. Let's not rush, hey."

"Alright, but you know I would like to kiss you right now."

"Yes, I want to kiss you."

I just embrace the moment and Frederick makes the first move, very very gently and slowly our lips make contact.

At first little peck-like kisses and gradually, as time passes by, becoming prolonged and heavy. In those few moments and the longing of wanting to and waiting very patiently but determined that he was to make the first move this time, I now know that this is the correct way to go with Frederick. I need him to want me as much as I want him. We are releasing passion which has obviously been building up over the past months.

Realising that the music has stopped I open my eyes, only to see that Frederick still has his eyes closed. I gently pull my lips away and Frederick slowly opens his eyes.

"The music has stopped," I mention.

"Oh so it has, I didn't realise."

Frederick walks over to the music centre and switches it off. He returns to me and put his arms around my shoulders.

"Now where were we? Oh yes, I remember."

Before I have time to answer we resume kissing until I gently pull my lips away and whisper, "Could we resume this in your bedroom?" followed by a quick, "Please."

"Are you sure, Melissa?"

"Yes, I am sure."

He gently takes my hand and leads me up to his bedroom.

After a few blissful hours of passionate lovemaking we lay side by side, bearing big smiley faces. He studies my face and I study his. I just want to stay in this moment forever.

"Melissa, my dear, dear lady, would you like some dessert now?"

"You didn't tell me what it is."

"Oh, right, well it's Eton Mess."

"Oh, go on then, yes, yes I do."

Frederick goes downstairs. I can see that there are only a couple of hours until I have to catch the last train back to Peaty Marsh. So when Frederick returns from the kitchen I am nearly dressed. He leaves a portion of Eton Mess for me on a nearby dressing table. He sits on the bed close to me.

"The last train back goes in a couple of hours so I need to get dressed."

"Oh, what a shame, and I was just enjoying our time together."

"So was I."

"Stay."

"I would really like to but there are things I need to do. Hum, I really enjoyed your Eton Mess. It was lovely. Thank you."

"You're welcome. Would you like a coffee before you go?"

"Yes I'd love a latte. Thank you."

I follow Frederick down to the kitchen.

"I've arranged for James to take you to the station, he'll be collecting you from The Guest House. I've wrapped the stems of your posy so you won't get your hands and clothes damp. I've just got to go back upstairs, there's something I need to get. When the green light is showing on the coffee machine just choose the type of coffee you want. Could you choose an espresso for me, please?"

"Bless you Frederick, as always you think of everything. You're my perfect man."

"Oh, I don't see myself as being perfect, far from it. Excuse me for a minute."

I go into the conservatory and I sit on the settee, sipping my coffee and looking out of the window. It is so peaceful. Frederick was now at his music centre, choosing a CD from his vast collection. He chose an orchestral piece of music. He came over to where I'm sitting and knelt before me, taking my left hand and making eye contact.

"Melissa, will you marry me?"

"I never expected this. What an unexpected surprise."

"Will you? Will you marry me, Melissa?"

"Of course I would like to, of course I will, but there are lots of things that I need to think about. I will need some time to think this over. Marriage is quite a serious issue with me. We haven't talked about where we will live, my job or anything. We will need to discuss this further and if I'm to catch that last train home I will need to start walking now-ish."

"I just want you to know how I truly feel about you and I want you to know that I want to spend the rest of my life with you. I was hoping that you'd come and live here at The Mound, here in my cottage. Take all the time you need, I'll wait."

"You've obviously had more time to think about us, marriage, etcetera, I had no idea. We haven't known each other for long either. We don't know yet if we can live under the same roof either. Up to now we've only spent some weekends together and it hasn't been every weekend so how do we know?"

"Melissa, I don't have all the answers to your questions. If we're going to be together then we do have to be practical and that will mean you leaving your job. You know you could get a teaching post, here at The Mound. There is a primary school and a boarding school so couldn't you transfer and work locally?"

Frederick took a few moments to gather his thoughts. I'm mulling over what he's just told me so there is a stony silence falling between us.

"If you don't want to marry me just yet then perhaps we could live together here and find out more about each other together. You're probably afraid of the commitment of marriage. I do understand, Melissa, if that's how you feel. Let's face it, I didn't know if I'd ever find or love anyone again, but I have, and it's you!"

"Yes, I know a lot has happened in the last few months and I feel that I need a bit more time to really think things over. Let's not rush."

"Yes alright, if that's how you feel. I'll just get clothed and I'll walk with you to The Guest House. If that's alright?"

"Yes, Frederick, that will be lovely."

Our eyes meet, we kiss and cuddle each other and the problems in my world, at least, seem to just melt away.